THE
GIRLIE POP
MURDER
CLUB

THE GIRLIE POP MURDER CLUB

The Girlie Pop Murders
Book One

EMBER EAST
WITH
CALLIOPE ZETSUBŌ

Interior Formatting & Design by Ember East
Cover by Ember East
Interior Images designed by Ember East

Warning:
This counts as evidence.
Read quickly, then burn.

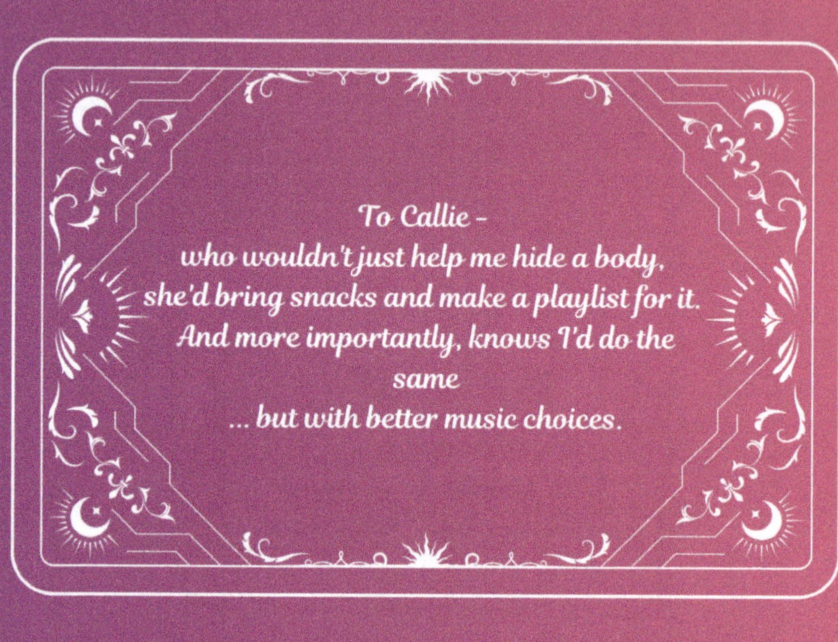

To Callie –
who wouldn't just help me hide a body,
she'd bring snacks and make a playlist for it.
And more importantly, knows I'd do the same
... but with better music choices.

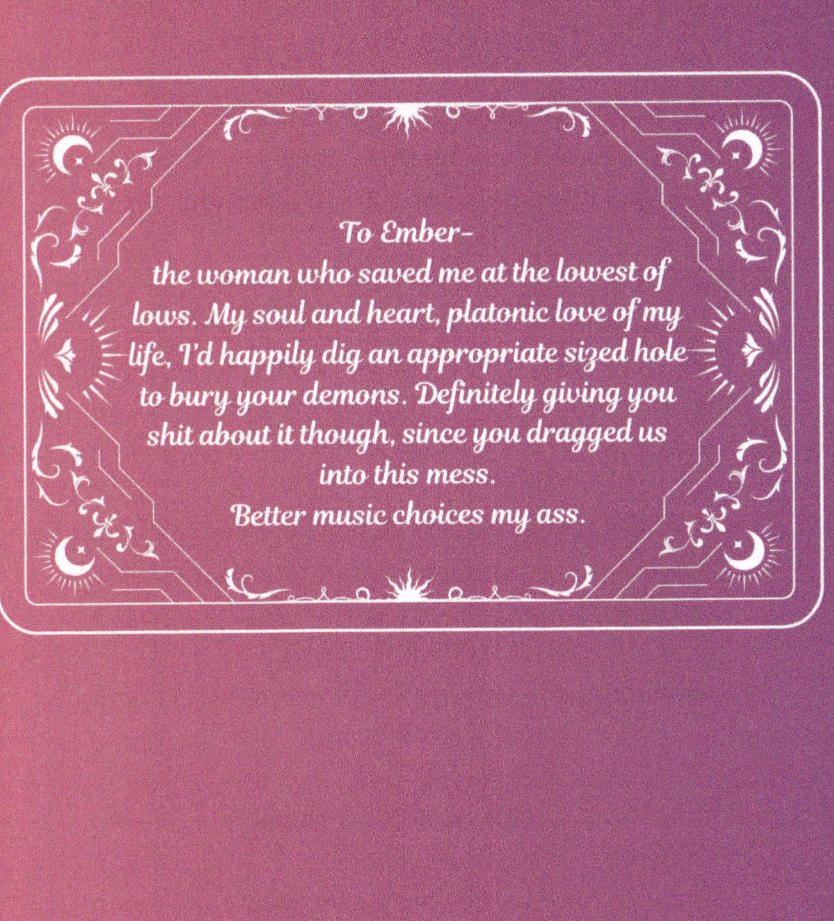

To Ember-
the woman who saved me at the lowest of
lows. My soul and heart, platonic love of my
life, I'd happily dig an appropriate sized hole
to bury your demons. Definitely giving you
shit about it though, since you dragged us
into this mess.
Better music choices my ass.

Trigger Warning:

Look, bestie. This book contains murder. Like, a lot of murder. Premeditated, sometimes poorly executed (pun intended), entirely justified murder.

If you're looking for a cozy mystery where everyone lives and learns valuable lessons, this ain't it. This is about bad men who make worse decisions, and the girlies who decide that murder is cheaper than therapy.

IMPORTANT STATISTIC THAT SHOULDN'T EXIST:
On average, nearly 20 people per minute are physically abused by an intimate partner in the United States.
1 in 4 women experience severe intimate partner physical violence.
More than 1 in 3 women experience sexual violence in their lifetime.

This book is for them.

(And also for anyone who's ever wanted to commit murder but settled for writing angry Yelp reviews instead. We see you. We appreciate your restraint. But also... have you considered investing in a Jeep?)

Note: No actual men were harmed in the writing of this book.

PLAYLIST

Got it Bad
- Daisy Grenade

We R Who We R
- Kesha

White Girl Wasted
- Kelly Paige

Are You Scared of Me Yet?
- Daisy Grenade

How to Hide A Body
- Daisy Grenade

Cannibal
- Kesha

Dead Men Don't Rape
- Delilah Bon

Goddess
- Xana

Bloody Mary
- Lady Gaga

I Am Not A Woman, I'm A God
- Halsey

Dead!
- My Chemical Romance

Die Young
- Kesha

Bad Guy
- Billie Eilish

Bonus:
Bubblegum Bitch
- Marina

EMBER'S NOTE

This novella crawled out of my brain after binge-watching Jennifer's Body, Heathers, and Legally Blonde in the same weekend (which, in retrospect, was basically my villain origin story). It's what happens when you take Elle Woods' determination, Veronica Sawyer's moral compass, and Jennifer Check's appetite for men, then add a dash of Sweeney Todd's way with sharp objects and a sprinkle of Mean Girls' aesthetic.

Musically, this story was fueled by a concerning amount of The Chicks' "Goodbye Earl" (the OG murder bestie anthem), Daisy Grenade's "How to Hide a Body" (which is suspiciously specific), and Delilah Bon's "Dead Men Don't Rape" (no lies detected).

But more than anything, this story is a love letter to my best friend and platonic soulmate, Calliope. She's the Wren to my Riley, minus the actual murder (as far as you know). She's the kind of friend who'd not only help me get away with murder but would turn it into an adventure, crime podcast references and perfectly timed inappropriate jokes. More importantly, she's the kind of friend who inspires you to write about murder because she understands that sometimes the best way to process trauma is through fictional revenge fantasies and dark humor.

This book is also inspired by all the women throughout history who decided that justice is best served... permanently. Women like:

- Marcia Kilgore, who killed her abusive husband and inspired country songs
- Ruth Ellis, who shot her abusive boyfriend and looked fabulous doing it
- Francine Hughes, who said "enough" with gasoline and a match
- Lorena Bobbitt, who... well, you know what she did
- The women of the "Murder Board" in Chicago, who helped other women escape their abusers (sometimes permanently)
- Belle Gunness, who turned getting rid of bad men into a successful business model

To all the women who've ever thought about choosing violence: *this one's for you.*

(Legal disclaimer: This is not a how-to guide. Any similarity to actual murders is purely coincidental. Please don't actually hit anyone with your car... without a really good alibi.)

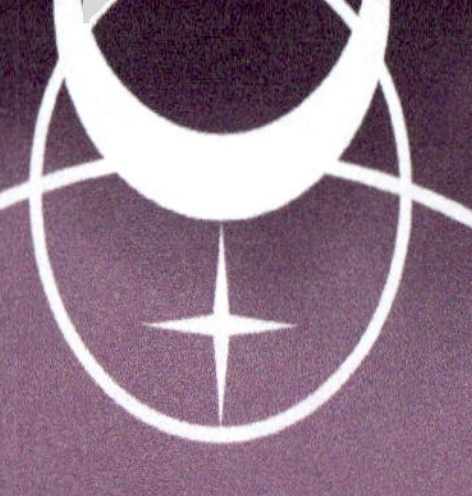

CALLIE'S NOTE

What can I say about how this book began other than pure chaos. The whirlwind of a human that is my best friend consumed a ton of media, and her mind took off. I love this girl with all my heart; she's the kind of best friend that you buy a house and raise kids with. So, when she popped the thought of this book into our unending chat stream, I happily let her pull me on board. Her determination to get me across the finish line into 'published author' territory is unmatched.

Co-writing this book with one of the few people I'd commit multiple felonies for is… cathartic, to say the least. Watching scenes play out, knowing her squirrel brain would absolutely hyperfocus on the vape she lost, while I constantly panic of DNA being left behind. She's the kind of person who will do anything for those she cares about, including writing a book with you about murder to process emotions

CONTENTS

PART ONE

ZERO TO MURDER IN
SIXTY SECONDS

"Um, bit of trivia, the human body
when drained of most of its blood
will oftentimes stop working."
-Woody Strode *Psych*

1
RiLEY

EX MARKS THE SPOT

November 1, 2014
2:30 AM

*I*f there was one thing Riley Thompson had learned in life, it was that burying a body was way harder than TV made it look. For starters, nobody ever mentioned the dirt. It got everywhere—under her nails, in her shoes, probably even in her lungs.

Huffing and puffing, she hauled herself out of the freshly dug pit, every muscle screaming in protest. She was coated head to toe in enough mud to make a spa therapist weep. Riley leaned on her shovel, glaring at her best friend Wren, who looked equally worse for wear on the other side of their makeshift grave.

"Okay," Riley wheezed, "next time, we're definitely hacking him up first."

Wren's head snapped up, her purple bangs plastered to her forehead. "Next time? We are not doing this again, Riley."

"Right," Riley replied, rolling her eyes. "Because Josh Bennet over there was our one-time-only, limited-edition murder special."

The man in question— or rather what was left of him— was lying in an awkward heap at the bottom of the hole. It had taken them a solid thirty minutes to roll him that far, with Riley nearly spraining something in the process and Wren collapsing into a fit of hysterical giggles about how they were the worst murderers in history. Now, his limbs were all tangled up in a way that didn't look natural, even for a dead guy.

"Why does he have to weigh, like, two hundred pounds?" Wren muttered, kicking at a clump of dirt. "I'm not built for this. I skipped leg day all last month."

"Yeah, and here we are, getting the best workout of our lives," Riley shot back, tossing her shovel aside with a clank. "Seriously, if we'd just chopped him up into bite-sized pieces, we wouldn't even be having this problem."

Wren winced. "Bite-sized? Could you not?"

Riley shrugged, reaching into her jacket pocket for her vape. She needed a break, a little puff of that artificial blueberry bliss. But her fingers came up empty. She froze, patted the other pocket, then rifled through her bag.

It wasn't there.

"Uh, Wren?" she said slowly, her tone laced with a growing dread. "You haven't seen my vape, have you?"

Wren's brow furrowed as she straightened up, wiping sweat from her forehead. "No… why?"

Riley's gaze drifted back to the freshly buried body. "Because I swear if I accidentally buried it with him, I'm digging it back up."

Her friend's horrified laugh echoed through the dark woods. "Please, tell me you're kidding."

Riley wasn't. But she was also too exhausted to actually start sifting through the dirt again. She sighed, pulling out her iPhone and swiping the screen on. The weak beam of the flashlight didn't do much to cut through the night, but it was enough to see the outline of her old Jeep Grand Cherokee parked in the distance. "Come on," she said, clapping her best friend on the shoulder. "Let's get back to the car before I start thinking of any more brilliant ideas."

The hike back was, unsurprisingly, just as grueling as the hike in, only now Riley's arms were aching from all the shoveling, and her mind was replaying the events of the past several hours in an endless loop, like a bad horror movie. She glanced at Wren, who was quietly trudging beside her.

"Remember when we thought college was going to be, like, frat parties and classes we didn't care about?" Riley mused aloud. "You know, instead of… whatever this is."

"Yeah," Wren replied, her tone dry. "I definitely

didn't see 'Burying Bodies 101' in the course catalog."

"Shame," Riley said, grinning. "I would've aced that class. Or at least, I would've aced the theory. The practical, maybe not so much."

As they finally reached the Jeep, they both collapsed into their seats, groaning in unison. Riley tilted her head back and stared at the ceiling. The overwhelming urge to find her vape was still gnawing at her, but there were more pressing matters to think about. At least if they ran into anyone they wouldn't question the blood on their clothes since it was Halloween. She glanced over at Wren, who was fiddling with the car keys in the driver's seat, her hands shaking just a little.

"Hey," Riley said, nudging her with an elbow. "You okay?"

"Fine," Wren replied, though her voice sounded distant. She turned the key, and the engine sputtered to life. "Just… trying to figure out if this is real life or a really messed-up fever dream."

"Well," Riley said, pulling down the visor to check her reflection in the mirror, "if it's a dream, then I'm definitely suing my subconscious for emotional distress."

As Wren pulled out onto the deserted road, Riley couldn't help but glance back toward the woods. Somewhere out there, Josh Bennet's final resting place was already being covered up by falling leaves. She just hoped that, wherever he was, her vape wasn't joining him on that eternal journey.

Because, really, she wasn't above going back and

digging it up if it came to that.

2
RiLEY

DAPHNE AND VELMA'S
BIG GAY HALLOWEEN

17 hours earlier...

Riley was not one to make a habit of being late. In fact, she prided herself on being that insufferably punctual friend who showed up early to everything and then texted "here" with annoying enthusiasm. But today was different. Today, she was sprinting across Riverside State University's quad like she was auditioning for a low-budget college remake of Chariots of Fire, her backpack bouncing against her spine and her Converse slapping against ancient cobblestones that were definitely not designed with running in mind.

Halloween or not, Professor Godwin's Linguistics

class waited for no one.

She glanced at her iPhone as she jogged, the time mocking her with its digital precision. "Dammit," she muttered, stuffing it back in her pocket.

Their tiny rental house – lovingly dubbed "The Shoebox" for its remarkable similarity to actual footwear storage – was a good twenty-minute walk from campus. This was a fact she'd completely disregarded when she'd hit snooze approximately seventeen times that morning, and now her lungs were staging a protest worthy of a union strike.

Her phone buzzed against her hip, and she yanked it out, answering without checking the caller ID because honestly, only one person would be calling to mock her tardiness right now. "Hello?" she wheezed, trying to sound less like she was about to collapse and more like she was casually exercising for fun.

"Where are you?" Wren's voice came through the line, managing to sound both concerned and deeply amused at the same time – a talent she'd perfected over their friendship.

"Uh, running," Riley replied, her breathlessness betraying any attempt at nonchalance. "Across campus. Trying to get to class before Professor Godwin decides I need a linguistics intervention. Or worse, makes me diagram sentences in front of everyone."

Wren snorted. "You're gonna give yourself a heart attack at this rate. Though I guess that would get you out of the midterm."

"Tell that to my lungs," Riley gasped, slowing to a jog as a group of students in matching Ghostbusters costumes ambled past, looking irritatingly relaxed about their academic commitments. "Seriously, I'm—" she paused, trying to catch her breath, "—almost there."

"Right," Wren said, her voice dripping with the kind of doubt usually reserved for pyramid schemes and dining hall mystery meat. "You're probably not even on the quad yet."

Riley stopped, glaring at a nearby tree as if it was personally responsible for her situation. "Hey, I'm at least halfway there. I can see the clock tower."

"Which means you're still five minutes away if you jog like you're being chased by a serial killer," Wren replied, her wit sharp enough to perform minor surgery. "Which, given your current breathing pattern, seems optimistic."

"Then I guess you'd better hope Josh isn't waiting outside your next class, huh?" Riley shot back before her brain could catch up with her mouth. The words hung in the air like expired Halloween candy – unwanted and slightly toxic.

There was a moment of silence on the other end of the line. Riley slowed her pace even more, mentally kicking herself. "Sorry," she added quickly. "That was… I didn't mean—"

"It's fine," Wren said, her tone lightening with practiced ease. "If Josh were smart enough to figure out my schedule, I'd be genuinely impressed. The man still thinks Mercury being in retrograde is a type of car problem."

"Guess that's too much to ask from a guy who thinks 'I'm sorry you feel that way' is an apology," Riley muttered, picking up her pace again. "Seriously, though. Has he been bothering you? Like, more than usual?"

"Only in the sense that he's still breathing," Wren replied dryly. "I've seen him around campus a couple of times. He doesn't really do anything, just… lingers. It's like he's trying to perfect the art of looking creepy. Should probably add that to his LinkedIn skills."

"Ugh." Riley felt a fresh wave of irritation surge through her. "Why does he still think he has a shot? He's about as charming as a wet sock. Actually, that's an insult to wet socks."

"More like a wet sock filled with rocks," Wren added. "And mold. And maybe some of that weird fungi that turns ants into zombies."

"Exactly," Riley said, finally reaching the top of the hill where the quad sloped down towards the Humanities building like a medieval torture device disguised as architecture. "Look, I'm almost there. Promise. Save me a seat in the back?"

"Already have," Wren replied. "I'll let Professor Godwin know you're running a little late. Maybe I'll tell him you're helping an old lady cross the street. That might win you some extra points for character development or something."

Riley laughed, finally reaching the building and slowing to a walk as she approached the steps. "Appreciate it. See you in a few."

She hung up and shoved her phone back into her pocket, her thoughts drifting to Josh as she took the stairs two at a time. It wasn't like he was dangerous—well, at least not in the obviously unhinged way. More like… persistent. The kind of guy who couldn't take a hint, even if you hired a plane to skywrite it across campus with a marching band accompaniment.

And Wren had tried everything short of that. She'd ended things weeks ago, and Josh's response had been a master class in textbook harassment, beginning by alternating between love-bombing texts and passive-aggressive comments about her social media posts. Then he started showing up at their house, Wren's work, and her classes.

It was like he thought if he just stood close enough to her orbit, she'd eventually pull him back in. Which was, honestly, about as likely as Professor Godwin showing up to class in a Halloween costume. Actually, now that she thought of it, that was far more likely to happen than Wren ever giving Josh the time of day again.

She burst through the door to the Linguistics lecture hall and spotted Wren sitting in their usual spot near the back, her purple hair like a beacon of salvation. Riley took a moment to catch her breath, giving Professor Godwin an apologetic nod as she slipped into the row next to her best friend.

"You made it," Wren whispered, sliding a large coffee towards her. "Just barely. Though I have to say, the whole 'just ran across campus' look really adds some casual messiness to your hair that you just couldn't accomplish organically."

"Never doubted me for a second," Riley whispered back, taking the cup and grinning. "And hey, at least I'm getting my cardio in before tonight's party."

The class passed in a blur of slides and notes, with Riley doing her best to jot down everything Professor Godwin said while simultaneously planning their Halloween costumes in the margins of her notebook. As the lecture drew to a close, he cleared his throat and turned his gaze toward the students, his gray beard practically bristling with the weight of impending wisdom.

"Before we call it a day," he announced, his voice echoing off the walls, "I have one last piece of advice. As many of you may know, there's a big party tonight over at the Omega Pi house, and I'd like to take this opportunity to remind you all that the legal drinking age is not an obstacle, it's a speed bump."

A wave of surprised laughter rippled through the room, and Professor Godwin continued, "So, be smart, and don't forget to use a designated driver if you're headed to the party. Otherwise, enjoy your Halloween, and try not to have too much fun. You're dismissed. And remember — the Great Vowel Shift was not, in fact, about someone stealing all the Es from English."

"Well," Wren said as they filed out of the room. "You're not going to the party, are you?"

"Of course I am, and so are you," Riley replied, glancing over her shoulder. "We need a night to just chill, right? Especially after all this Josh drama. I've already got our costumes planned."

"Oh, no," Wren groaned. "Last time you planned the costumes, we were the weirdest Powerpuff Girls the world has ever seen. Not to mention we didn't have a Blossom. We looked like we'd lost our leader in a tragic chemical X accident."

"That was a statement," Riley said, grinning. "About the inherent flaws in trio-based power structures."

"It was a mistake," Wren corrected. "Please, not two-thirds of the Powerpuff Girls again. My pride can't take another hit like that."

"Don't worry," Riley replied, nudging her shoulder. "These costumes are actually cool. We're going as Daphne and Velma."

"As in only two-fifths of the Scooby Gang? Do you see the running problem here?" Wren asked, her eyes narrowing. "We're developing a concerning pattern of incomplete group costumes."

"Come on," Riley whined, flashing her best pleading look – the one she'd perfected after years of convincing Wren to watch just one more episode of whatever show they were binging. "We don't need those guys, everyone knows Daphne and Velma were one of the original lesbian power couples."

"Okay, true," Wren admitted. "But, you're not trying to convince me, you're trying to convince yourself."

Riley opened her mouth to argue, then closed it, recognizing defeat when it wore purple hair and a knowing smirk. She shrugged. "Fine. You're right, and I'm a huge lesbian who wants to dress as Daphne. Happy?"

"Ecstatic," Wren said, grinning. "Now, let's go home and put these costumes together before I change my mind."

3
WREN

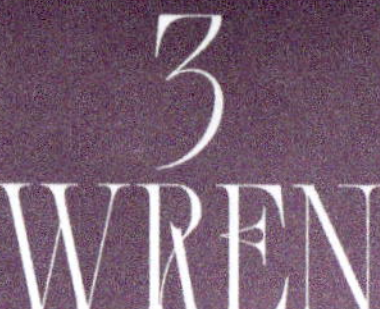

10:30 PM

The bass from the Halloween party thumped through the floorboards of the Omega Pi house, vibrating up through Wren's combat boots as she leaned against the wall. She was nursing a red Solo cup filled with what the frat boys optimistically called "punch" but was basically lighter fluid with food coloring. Through the crowd of costumed college students – most of whom had clearly raided the "Sexy [Insert Random Profession Here]" section at Party City – she could see Riley dancing, her Daphne costume's purple dress swishing as she moved to the music. The orange wig she'd insisted on wearing was slightly askew, making her look less like a cartoon detective and more like someone who'd lost a fight with a traffic cone.

Wren smiled behind her own cup, adjusting the thick-rimmed glasses that completed her Velma costume. She'd tried to convince Riley that they could've gone as something else – anything else – but once Riley got an idea in her head, there was no talking her out of it. It was like arguing with a golden retriever who'd decided your shoe was its new best friend.

"Go dance!" Riley had insisted earlier, practically shoving Wren away from their spot by the wall. "Stop being my shadow and have some fun!"

"I am having fun," Wren had protested. "I'm judging everyone's life choices. It's very fulfilling."

But truthfully, she was perfectly content where she was, watching her best friend light up the makeshift dance floor like she'd been born for it. That was the thing about Riley – she filled every space she entered, not in an overwhelming way, but like sunshine streaming through a window. Warm, bright, and impossible to ignore, even when she was doing wasn't what most would call dancing– maybe failing was the better term.

The sight triggered a memory: their first meeting in that tiny classroom back in freshman year, both of them the only ones who'd signed up for "Pop Culture in Media: The Buffy Effect." Wren had practically sprinted to class that day, arriving fifteen minutes early because who wouldn't be excited about analyzing Buffy for actual college credit? She'd been setting up her color-coded notes (organized by season, episode, and supernatural creature type, naturally) when in walked one other student – a tall blonde with space buns and a denim jacket covered in patches that read "Eat the Patriarchy" and "Girls just want to have FUNdamental rights."

"Guess we're the only ones with taste," Riley had said, grinning as she dropped into the seat next to Wren. "I mean, who doesn't want to watch Buffy and get college credit? Everyone else is probably off taking something useful, like Advanced Basket Weaving or The Philosophy of Reality TV."

"Their loss," Wren had replied, already sliding over her meticulously organized episode guide. "They'll never know the deep sociopolitical implications of why vampires can't wear leather pants."

The class had been canceled after that first session – apparently, two students weren't enough to justify keeping it on the schedule, which was clearly the university's loss.

But by then, it didn't matter. They'd spent those three hours analyzing "Welcome to the Hellmouth" and discovering they shared the same dry sense of humor, the same taste in music, and the same theory that Principal Snyder was actually a demon (which was later proven untrue, but at least his demise was satisfying.)

Sometimes Wren wondered if there was such a thing as platonic soulmates. Because that's what they were – two halves of the same whole, complementing each other's strengths and weaknesses like they'd been designed that way. Where Riley was bold and impulsive, Wren was cautious and calculating. When Wren retreated into herself, Riley knew exactly how to draw her back out. They were basically a buddy cop movie waiting to happen, minus the cops, plus a lot more takeout and true crime documentaries.

A pair of hands suddenly gripped her hips from behind, yanking her from her thoughts. Wren spun around, some of her drink sloshing over the rim of her cup, ready to tell off whoever thought they had the right to—

Josh.

Her stomach dropped at the sight of him, his familiar smirk making her skin crawl. He was dressed as some kind of demon, red face paint smeared across his features in what she assumed was supposed to be scary. Instead, it mainly looked like he'd face-planted into a cherry pie. (Notice how the red flags match his devil costume? That's called literary symbolism, kids.) His eyes were clear and focused. Too focused.

"Get your hands off me," Wren snapped, stepping back until she hit the wall. "I know personal space is a foreign concept to you, but maybe try Google Translate."

"Come on, baby," Josh said, his words slightly slurred. "Don't be like that. I've missed you."

"I'm not your baby," Wren's voice was ice. "And I told you to leave me alone. What part of that was unclear? Should I have used smaller words?"

He stepped closer, effectively boxing her in. "You

can't keep ignoring me forever. We were good together. You know we were."

"Good together?" Wren let out a harsh laugh. "Is that what you call monitoring my texts? Or showing up at my work unannounced? Or telling me what to wear? Because I've got to tell you, Josh, that's not exactly what I'd call relationship goals. More like the plot of a Lifetime movie, and not one of the good ones."

"I was looking out for you," Josh insisted, his expression darkening. "But you always have to make everything so dramatic."

"Oh, I'm sorry," Wren's voice dripped with sarcasm. "I didn't realize having basic boundaries was considered dramatic these days. My bad. Should I have just let you continue your audition for 'How to Lose a Girlfriend in Ten Days: Stalker Edition'?"

Her hand tightened around her cup, knuckles going white. She glanced toward the dance floor, but Riley was lost in the crowd now, probably unable to hear anything over the music anyway. The wall of bodies around them seemed to close in, making the air feel thick and heavy with the smell of cheap beer and even cheaper cologne.

"I'm leaving," Wren announced, ducking under Josh's arm. She needed air, needed space, needed to be anywhere but here, preferably somewhere with better ventilation and fewer ex-boyfriends with boundary issues.

"Wren, wait—" Josh reached for her arm, but she jerked away.

"Don't touch me," she hissed, pushing through

the crowd toward the door. She tried to spot Riley one last time, but the sea of costumes had become an indistinguishable blur of polyester and poor decisions. Pulling out her phone, she typed out a quick text.

Wren: Heading home. Josh being Josh. Don't worry, I'm fine. Though if you happen to know any good hitmen, I'm not opposed to exploring options.

The cool October air hit her face as she stepped outside, and Wren took a deep breath, letting it clear her head. Their rental house wasn't far — maybe ten minutes on foot. She'd walked it plenty of times before, usually with significantly less stalker-y company.

She'd barely made it down the front steps when she heard the door open behind her.

"So that's it?" Josh's voice carried across the front lawn. "You're just going to run away?"

Wren kept walking, faster now. The streets were relatively quiet for Halloween, most people were either at parties or done with trick-or-treating for the night. Leaves crunched under her boots as she moved, trying to focus on the sound instead of the footsteps she could hear behind her. It was like having the world's most persistent, annoying shadow.

"You know what your problem is?" Josh continued, his voice getting closer. "You think you're better than everyone else. Better than me."

"My problem," Wren shot back without turning around, "is that you can't take a hint. I mean, what part of 'leave me alone' sounds like 'please follow me home while monologuing like a B-movie villain'?"

"Oh, I got the hint," he sneered. "Little Miss Perfect decided I wasn't good enough for her anymore. Started telling people I was controlling, that I was toxic—"

"You ARE toxic!" The words burst out of her before she could stop them. "You're manipulative and possessive and, honestly? The red flags you're waving could supply a small communist parade."

"I LOVED YOU!" The raw anger in his voice made her flinch. "Everything I did was because I loved you, but you're too stuck up to see that. Too busy playing the victim—"

"Following me home right now isn't exactly helping your case," Wren pointed out, relief flooding through her as she spotted their house at the end of the street. Just a little further. "In fact, I'd say it's pretty much the textbook definition of proving my point."

"Following you?" Josh let out a bitter laugh. "Maybe I just happen to be going this way. Maybe you're not as important as you think you are."

"Right," Wren muttered under her breath. "Because nothing says 'you're not important' like stalking someone home while providing running commentary."

She reached their front walkway, fishing her keys out of her pocket with trembling fingers. The porch light was on – they always left it on when they were out – casting long shadows across the lawn.

"You need to get over yourself," Josh was saying, his voice carrying from the end of the path where he'd stopped. "You're not special, Wren. You're just a stuck-up bitch who—"

Wren spun around, fury finally overwhelming her fear. "You want to know what I am, Josh? I'm done. Done with your games, done with your manipulation, done with—"

The rest of her words were cut off by the sudden screech of tires. Wren turned just in time to see Riley's Jeep come flying around the corner, headlights cutting through the darkness like laser beams. Everything seemed to slow down, like a movie going frame by frame:

The look of confusion on Josh's face as he turned toward the sound.

The determined set of Riley's jaw, visible through the windshield.

The sickening thud as two tons of metal collided with flesh and bone.

Then, silence…

And that's why you don't monologue on someone's front lawn.

4
WREN

SO, YOU'VE COMMITTED MANSLAUGHTER: A BEGINNER'S GUIDE

11:00 P.M.

Wren stood frozen on her front lawn, staring at the scene before her like a particularly morbid art installation. The Jeep's headlights cut through the fog, illuminating Josh's crumpled form in harsh relief against the pavement. His devil costume seemed oddly appropriate now, though the plastic horns had snapped off on impact and skittered across the street like rejected props from a low grade horror movie.

"Oh god," Riley's voice cracked from inside the Jeep. "Oh god, oh god, oh god."

Wren's brain seemed to be buffering, stuck

somewhere between blind panic and hysterical laughter. Because really, of all the ways she'd imagined this night ending, watching her best friend turn her ex-boyfriend into roadkill hadn't even made the top ten.

Riley's hands were still gripping the steering wheel so tightly her knuckles had gone white, her chest heaving with rapid, shallow breaths. A thin trickle of blood ran from her nose where she'd hit the steering wheel, making her look like she'd tried to french kiss a brick wall.

"Riley," Wren managed, her own voice sounding distant and strange. "Riley, you need to breathe."

"I am breathing!" Riley gasped, which was technically true in the same way a fish flopping on deck was technically swimming. "I'm breathing so much! All the breathing! I just—I didn't mean to—oh god, is he dead? Please tell me he's not dead. Maybe he's just taking a really dramatic nap?"

Wren forced herself to look at Josh's body again. The angle of his neck answered that question pretty definitively. "Let's just say he won't be stalking anyone else's front lawn anytime soon."

That was apparently the wrong thing to say, because Riley's breathing kicked up another notch, edging into territory usually reserved for marathon runners or particularly enthusiastic hamsters. "I killed him. Oh my god, I killed him. I'm a murderer. I'm going to go to jail, and they don't even have good coffee in jail, Wren. It's all instant! I can't drink instant coffee!"

"Okay, first of all," Wren said, reaching through the

open window to grab Riley's chin, tilting it up to examine her bloody nose, "your priorities are concerning. And second, you're not going to jail because we're not going to get caught. Now breathe with me before you pass out and make this night even more complicated."

She dabbed at Riley's nose with the sleeve of her Velma sweater, which was probably ruined anyway. The whole "solving mysteries" aesthetic had taken on a darker turn than Hanna-Barbera probably intended.

"In and out," Wren coached, trying to keep her own voice steady despite the tremor in her hands. "Come on, you know how to breathe, right? It's that thing you do all the time when you're not having an existential crisis in my driveway."

Riley's breathing slowly began to even out, though her eyes remained wide and glassy. "I just—I saw him coming at you, and I panicked. I thought maybe if I just scared him a little..."

"Well," Wren said dryly, "I'd say mission accomplished. He looks pretty scared to me. Also very dead, but definitely scared."

"Not helping!"

"Right, sorry." Wren released Riley's chin and started pacing along the sidewalk, her mind racing. "Okay, we need to think this through. What are our options?"

"Call the police?" Riley suggested weakly.

"Oh sure, great idea. 'Hello, officer? Sorry to bother you on Halloween, but my best friend just turned my stalker ex into a hood ornament. No, that's not a decoration, that's actually him. Yes, the devil costume is real. No, the irony is not lost on us.'" Wren ran her hands through her hair, messing up her carefully styled Velma look. "Try again."

"We could... say it was an accident?" Riley ventured. "Like, maybe he was dressed as a speed bump and I just didn't see him?"

Wren stopped pacing to stare at her. "A speed bump. On Halloween. In a devil costume."

"Okay, fine, maybe he tripped and fell in front of the car?"

"Right, because people regularly trip and fall directly into oncoming vehicles that just happen to be driven by their ex-girlfriend's best friend." Wren resumed her pacing with renewed vigor. "No, we need something else. Something that doesn't end with both of us sharing a cell with someone named Big Bertha who collects toenail clippings."

They both looked at Josh's body, still illuminated by the headlights like the world's most unfortunate spotlight. A cat wandered past, took one look at the scene, and promptly decided it wanted nothing to do with whatever was happening here. Smart cat.

"We need to move him," Wren decided, the words coming out before she'd fully processed them. "We can't leave him out here like this. Mrs. Henderson next door is notorious for her 3 AM 'check the neighborhood for suspicious activity' walks, and I really don't want to explain to her why there's a dead guy accessorizing my driveway."

Riley nodded slowly, finally releasing her death grip on the steering wheel. "Right. Okay. Moving the body. That's... that's a thing we're doing now. Cool. Cool cool cool. Totally normal Halloween activity."

They approached Josh's body like cats being dragged to a bath - slowly, regretfully, and with serious consideration of running in the opposite direction. Up close, he looked even more ridiculous – the cheap red face paint had smeared across the pavement, making him look less like a devil and more like a finger painting gone wrong. At least, Wren hoped that was red face paint on the side walk and not something more…incriminating.

"On three?" Wren suggested, grabbing his shoulders while Riley took his feet. "One, two—"

"Holy shit, why is he so heavy?" Riley wheezed as they tried to lift him. "What was he eating, concrete?"

"Well, he always did have a thick skull," Wren grunted, readjusting her grip. "Though I guess that didn't help much in the end."

They managed to drag him a few feet before having to stop and catch their breath. His demon tail scraped against the pavement, an awkward sound that pierced the silence of the night and made both girls cringe.

"Great," Wren muttered, blowing her purple bangs out of her face. "Now he's going to haunt us as a devil for sure. As if regular ghost Josh wouldn't be annoying enough."

"Maybe if he wasn't wearing fifteen layers of toxic masculinity under that costume, he'd be lighter," Riley muttered, then clapped a hand over her mouth. "Oh god, I'm stress-joking about a dead body. This is it. This is my villain origin story."

"Well, you did just commit vehicular manslaughter, so I'd say your moral compass might need some recalibrating." Wren adjusted her grip again. "Come on, the garage is just a few more feet. Unless you'd rather leave him here as a very convincing Halloween decoration?"

With much grunting, cursing, and one particularly memorable moment where Josh's arm flopped out and nearly gave Riley a heart attack, they finally managed to drag him into the garage. The door closed behind them with a thud that seemed to echo with finality.

They stood there in the dim light, staring at the body of Wren's ex-boyfriend, who was currently doing an excellent impression of a broken mannequin on their garage floor. The reality of the situation seemed to hit them both at once.

"Oh my god," Riley whispered, sliding down to sit on an old crate. "Oh my god, we killed him. We actually killed him."

"Technically, you killed him," Wren corrected, running her hands through her hair again. "I'm just an accessory after the fact. Which, by the way, is not something I ever thought I'd have to specify."

"This isn't happening," Riley continued, her voice rising in pitch. "This can't be happening. Maybe we're both having a really weird shared hallucination? Maybe someone spiked the punch at the party?"

"If this is a hallucination, it's a very detailed one," Wren replied, pacing between the lawn mower and the recycling bins. "Complete with realistic body weight and everything. Also, you didn't even drink the punch."

"Because it looked like nuclear waste!"

"Not really the point right now!"

They stared at each other for a long moment, their breathing loud in the enclosed space. Josh's body lay between them like the world's most awkward conversation starter.

"What are we supposed to do now?" Riley asked, her voice small. "I mean, we can't just leave him here. Eventually someone's going to notice the smell, and I really don't want to explain to my professors why my garage smells like eau de dead ex-boyfriend."

Wren ran her hands over her face, smearing what was left of her makeup. "Okay, okay, we need to think this through. Step by step. Like a... like a wikihow article. 'How to Handle a Dead Ex-Boyfriend in 10 Steps or Less.'"

"I don't think wikihow covers this sort of thing."

"Well, maybe they should!" Wren threw her hands up. "It would be a lot more useful than 'How to Train Your Cat to Play Chess' or whatever other useless articles they have."

Riley looked like she was about to argue, then paused. "Wait, can you actually train a cat to play chess?"

"Not the time, Riley!"

"Right, sorry." Riley took a deep breath, then

suddenly sat up straighter. "Oh god, what about cameras? Are there any security cameras around here?"

They both froze, then simultaneously looked toward Mrs. Henderson's house. The old woman was notorious for her paranoia about neighborhood security.

"No," Wren said slowly, thinking it through. "She has a doorbell camera, but it only points at her front porch. And this street is too residential for traffic cams." She let out a shaky laugh. "I guess this is one time we can be thankful for our neighborhood's lack of proper surveillance."

"Small mercies," Riley muttered, then glanced at Josh again. "So... what now?"

Wren looked around the garage, taking inventory of their resources. "Well, we have some garbage bags, a shovel from when we tried to start that garden last spring—"

"You mean when you killed those tomato plants?"

"They were defective tomatoes and you know it." Wren shot her a look. "The point is, we have some basic supplies. We just need to figure out where to... um..."

"Hide the body?" Riley supplied helpfully.

"I was going to say 'relocate our unexpected guest,' but sure, let's just jump straight to murder terminology. Why not? We've already committed the crime, might as well use the vocabulary."

They both fell silent again, the weight of their situation settling over them like a particularly morbid blanket. Through the garage's small window, Wren could see the moon hanging low and full in the sky, as if it was trying to get a better look at their predicament.

"You know what the worst part is?" Riley said suddenly, her voice taking on that slightly hysterical edge again. "I'm pretty sure I still have class tomorrow morning."

Wren stared at her for a long moment, then burst out laughing. She couldn't help it – the absurdity of the situation, the adrenaline – it all came bubbling up in a wave of inappropriate hilarity.

Riley joined in after a moment, and soon they were both doubled over, tears streaming down their faces as they laughed like maniacs in their garage at 11:30 on Halloween, with the corpse of Wren's ex-boyfriend serving as their unwitting audience.

"We're going to hell," Riley gasped between giggles. "We are absolutely going to hell."

"Well," Wren replied, wiping her eyes and smearing her glasses in the process, "at least Josh can give us directions."

5
RiLEY

11:30 P.M.

Riley was discovering that murder left you with a lot of awkward downtime. Like now, sitting in their garage in blood-stained Halloween costumes, sharing a joint rolled in her favorite strawberry-flavored papers, while a dead body cooled not ten feet away. The whole scene had a surreal quality to it, like a true crime documentary directed by Wes Anderson.

The garage was dimly lit by a single bulb that buzzed intermittently, casting strange shadows on the concrete floor. Their wigs lay discarded nearby – the orange Daphne disaster and the short brown Velma bob looking like abandoned pets. Riley took another hit from the joint, watching the smoke curl up toward the ceiling. The familiar smell barely masked the other, more concerning odors Riley could swear were beginning to permeate the space.

"You know what I've always hated?" Riley said suddenly, breaking the heavy silence that had settled between them. "Those creepy porcelain dolls. The ones people keep on shelves? Just… staring at you with their dead little eyes, like they're mentally cataloging all the ways they could murder you in your sleep."

Wren, who had been absently picking dried blood from under her fingernails, looked up with an expression that suggested she was seriously reconsidering their friendship. "Okay… and what exactly brought that up?"

"Nothing really," Riley shrugged, gesturing vaguely with the joint. "Just thinking how this whole situation has the same vibe. Like, we're being judged by some dead guy wearing plastic devil horns. It's kind of poetic if you think about it. Which I have been. A lot."

"Right," Wren drawled, reaching for the joint. "Because that's definitely what we should be focusing on right now. Not the very real, very dead ex-boyfriend in my parents' old tarp."

"To be fair," Riley pointed out, "he's technically not your ex-boyfriend anymore. He's more like… your ex-person." She paused, considering. "Your ex-existence?"

"Please stop helping."

Riley held up her hands in surrender, then

immediately ruined it by adding, "I'm just saying, semantics are important in situations like this. I think. I don't actually have much experience with post-murder terminology."

"That's… reassuring, I guess?" Wren sat forward in her chair, which creaked ominously. "But we need to focus. We need a plan."

"I have a plan," Riley offered brightly. "Step one: don't panic. Step two: panic anyway, but quietly."

"A real plan," Wren insisted, though her lips twitched. "We need to figure out how to… dispose of him." She gestured toward the tarp-wrapped bundle that had once been Josh Bennet, local creep and current inconvenience.

"Right," Riley nodded, trying to match Wren's serious tone. "Disposal. Like Marie Kondo, but for bodies. Does he spark joy? No? Into the trash he goes."

"Riley."

"Sorry, sorry." Riley sat up straighter, attempting to focus despite the pleasant haziness in her head. "Okay, so we need to wrap him up better. Maybe garbage bags? To prevent any…" she waggled her fingers, searching for a delicate way to put it, "…leakage."

"Gross, but yes." Wren stood up, starting to pace. "And we need somewhere to… put him. There's this old farm about twenty minutes out of town. It's like two hundred acres, mostly woods. The farmer who owns it is ancient – probably hasn't checked the back portion in years."

"Or," Riley said slowly, a thought forming through

the THC fog, "we could take him down to the lake area near the national park. There's all that abandoned land out there, and I know this spot – there's this old unmarked graveyard. Nobody ever goes there."

Wren stopped pacing and stared at her friend. The silence stretched for a long moment before she finally asked, "Where the hell did you come up with that? That was… disturbingly specific."

Riley shrugged, aiming for nonchalant but probably hitting somewhere closer to suspicious. "I'm resourceful?"

"Yeah, that's not concerning at all." Wren shook her head, but she was already moving around the garage, gathering supplies. She grabbed a roll of heavy-duty garbage bags from under the workbench, followed by duct tape and two rusty shovels that had previously only seen action in their failed attempt at a vegetable garden. "We need to move fast. The longer we wait, the more likely someone will…" She trailed off, apparently unable to finish that particular thought.

Riley watched her friend's efficient movements, a strange sense of calm settling over her. Maybe it was the weed, or maybe it was the lingering adrenaline, but everything felt weirdly… manageable. Like they were just tackling another college project, except instead of analyzing Shakespeare, they were disposing of a body. Same difference, really. Both involved a lot of death.

"You know what we should do first?" Riley asked, finally standing up and stretching. Her Daphne costume, now stiff with dried blood, crackled with the movement.

"We should stop by Walgreens."

Wren froze, a coil of rope in her hands. "What? You want to stop at Walgreens. While we have a dead body in the Jeep?"

"Yeah, I need a new vape."

Riley hadn't expected there to be so many errands involved with her first murder experience. Yet here she was, pulling into a Walgreens parking lot at midnight, still wearing a blood-spattered Daphne costume, about to shop for snacks and supplies like this was just another late-night study session. Except instead of cramming for finals, they were preparing to bury a body. Same stress levels, though.

"This is literally the worst idea you've ever had," Wren muttered as Riley killed the engine. "And I'm including the time you tried to convince me we could pass our entire Spanish final by only speaking in SpongeBob quotes."

"Hey, that would've worked if Professor Martinez had a better sense of humor," Riley protested, checking her reflection in the rearview mirror. Most of the blood on her face had dried to a flattering shade of rust. "Besides, we need supplies. And I need nicotine. And you need to stop looking like you're about to throw up, because that's definitely going to attract attention."

Wren took a deep breath, her hands still gripping the steering wheel like it might try to escape. "Fine. But we're making this quick. Get your vape, get some garbage bags, and let's go. No wandering around like it's a normal shopping trip."

"Of course not," Riley agreed solemnly. "This is clearly an abnormal shopping trip."

The fluorescent lights inside Walgreens felt harsh after the darkness of their garage, making Riley squint as they grabbed a basket. The store was nearly empty, save for a bored-looking cashier scrolling through their phone, and a couple of drunk college kids arguing over which flavor of Doritos was superior. (Cool Ranch, obviously, but Riley had more pressing matters to attend to).

She made a beeline for the vape section, scanning the options before grabbing her usual blueberry flavor. Behind her, Wren was methodically collecting what she called "practical items" – garbage bags, duct tape, protein bars, and water. Always the responsible one, even during felonies.

"Ooh, look!" Riley exclaimed, holding up a package of face paint from the Halloween clearance section. "We could do camouflage. You know, really commit to this whole military-style operation thing we've got going."

Wren's expression could have frozen Hell over. "We are trying to not look like we're about to commit a felony. Put the face paint down."

"But it's on sale!"

"Riley."

"Fine," Riley sighed, dropping it back on the shelf. "But I'm getting these gummy bears. We're gonna need energy for all the manual labor in our immediate future." She tossed several bags into their basket, along with some chips and energy drinks. "What? Digging is hard work. I assume. I don't actually have much experience in that department. Yet."

They approached the checkout counter, trying to look as normal as possible – which, given that they were still in bloody Halloween costumes, was a relative term. The cashier barely glanced up from their phone, scanning their items with the enthusiasm of someone who had seen far worse on the Halloween night shift.

Back in the car, Riley immediately lit up her new vape, the familiar cloud of blueberry-scented vapor filling the space. "See?" she said, exhaling. "That wasn't so bad. No one even asked why we needed industrial-strength garbage bags at midnight."

"Probably because we look like we just came from a horror movie," Wren pointed out, starting the engine.

"Which, technically, we kind of did."

The drive to the lake area was filled with an awkward silence that Riley couldn't help but fill. She fiddled with the radio, eventually landing on a late-night talk show discussing Halloween urban legends. "Oh, how appropriate," she commented. "Nothing like some ghost stories to accompany our totally normal midnight drive."

"With our totally normal trunk passenger," Wren added dryly.

"Exactly!" Riley grinned, taking another hit from her vape. "Although I guess Josh is more likely to become an urban legend than see one at this point." She paused. "Too soon?"

"Considering he's still technically in the car with us? Yes."

They fell into random conversation after that, carefully avoiding any mention of their current situation. Riley told stories about their disaster of a Spanish final, about the time they tried to start a band despite neither of them playing instruments, about anything that would keep their minds off the very real consequences of what they were doing.

"Oh hey," Riley said suddenly, reaching over to poke Wren. "Put your seatbelt on. The last thing we need is to get pulled over for a safety violation while we're committing several major felonies. Like, imagine trying to explain that to a cop. 'Sorry officer, just taking our dead friend for a scenic drive. Don't mind the suspicious tarp in the back.'"

They both laughed, but it had an edge of hysteria to it. The kind of laughter that comes when the alternative is screaming.

Finally, they pulled up to the secluded area near the lake where Riley remembered the old graveyard being located. The headlights swept across ancient trees before Wren killed the engine, plunging them into darkness broken only by moonlight filtering through the branches.

"Time for a costume change," Riley announced, pulling out the black clothes they'd brought along. "Although I have to say, going from Scooby-Doo to cat burglar is a weird career progression."

They changed quickly, though Riley kept getting tangled in her dress in her haste to get it off. "This is why Daphne always got caught by the bad guys," she muttered, finally freeing herself. "Can't run from monsters in this thing."

The real challenge came when they opened the trunk. Josh's body, wrapped in the tarp and garbage bags, looked somehow larger than Riley remembered. "Okay," she said, taking one last hit from her vape for courage. "Let's get this over with before I start thinking too hard and run away screaming."

Moving a dead body, as it turned out, was nothing like the movies made it look. It was awkward, heavy, and involved a lot more cursing. They almost dropped him twice, and at one point, Riley was pretty sure she pulled something in her shoulder.

"Why," she grunted as they navigated through

the trees, "didn't we think to bring a wheelbarrow or something? Or at least pick a smaller victim?"

"Because we're new at this," Wren replied through gritted teeth. "And it wasn't exactly a planned event."

They only got lost once, taking a wrong turn at a fork in the trail that led them to an old, collapsed shed. "Hey," Riley said brightly as they backtracked, "we only got lost once. That's basically a flawless victory for us. Although," she added thoughtfully, "I guess Josh doesn't get a vote in our navigation skills anymore."

The old graveyard, when they finally reached it, looked exactly as creepy as Riley remembered. Weathered headstones stuck out of the ground at odd angles, surrounded by overgrown weeds and gnarled trees that looked like they belonged in a Tim Burton movie.

"Well," Riley said, dropping her end of the tarp with a thud, "time to dig. And here I thought my workout routine was intense before."

The actual digging proved to be the worst part. The ground was hard and rocky, and every shovelful felt like it weighed a ton. They took turns, one digging while the other kept watch, though Riley wasn't sure what exactly they were watching for. Zombie apocalypse, maybe?

"I just hope we're not accidentally digging someone else up," Riley commented, pausing to wipe sweat from her forehead. "That would be the definition of bad karma."

"Or we're giving them a roommate," Wren replied. "Either way, not ideal."

"Yeah, pretty sure 'good roommate matching' isn't in

the graveyard's amenities package."

After what felt like several centuries but was probably closer to two hours, they finally had a hole that looked deep enough. Wren suggested making the hole tube-shaped rather than a traditional grave, so when the grass grew back, it would leave only a small circular mark instead of a body-sized outline.

She stood in it to check, declaring, "Well, it's either six feet or we're both shorter than we thought."

Getting Josh into the hole was another adventure in awkward maneuvering and creative cursing. Riley was pretty sure she invented several new swear words in the process. Finally, though, he was in, and they began the equally arduous task of covering him up.

"You know," Riley said as they patted down the dirt with their shovels, trying to make it look less obviously disturbed, "I really didn't expect murder to involve this much manual labor. They never show this part in the crime shows."

"Probably because watching people dig for two hours isn't great television," Wren pointed out.

"Fair point. Although I think we could make it work. Add some dramatic music, maybe a montage..."

[Cue "Dead!" by My Chemical Romance]

...Wren and Riley taking turns with the shovel, their movements becoming increasingly dramatic and synchronized, like a particularly morbid ballet...

...Riley pausing to take a vape break, accidentally blowing a perfect smoke ring that forms a halo above

Josh's burial site…

…Wren meticulously arranging leaves over the disturbed earth while Riley poses dramatically in the background with her shovel like she's shooting an album cover…

…Both girls simultaneously wiping sweat from their foreheads with the back of their hands, leaving identical streaks of dirt across their faces…

…Riley attempting to time her shovel strikes to the beat of imaginary background music, while Wren watches with an expression that clearly says "I can't take you anywhere, not even to bury a body"…

…A raccoon wandering past, taking one look at their operation, and immediately turning around like it decided to quit being nocturnal…

…Both girls frozen mid-shovel as a car passes in the distance, looking like the world's most suspicious garden enthusiasts…

…Riley practicing her alibi facial expressions while Wren actually does the work, cycling through "surprised," "concerned," and "I definitely didn't kill anyone" before settling on "mildly constipated"…

[Music fades]

"You know," Riley said, leaning on her shovel like it was a cane at a particularly casual funeral, "I think we really nailed that montage. Though maybe we should've gone with 'Another One Bites the Dust' instead."

"I'm disowning you," Wren replied, but she was fighting a smile. "Right now. In this graveyard. Seems appropriate."

Evidence
January 13, 2015
Case Number 27b57
Detective: W.W.

01-15

7
WREN

4:00 AM

Mud masks weren't designed with murder in mind. The green clay was already starting to crack around Wren's mouth, probably from all the nervous lip-biting she'd been doing since they got home. She'd chosen the "detoxifying" mask because it seemed appropriate— if anything needed detoxifying right now, it was her conscience.

Beside her on their threadbare couch, Riley was sprawled out in her "Team Edward" pajama shirt, which had seen better days (much like Josh, though at least the shirt hadn't been hit by a car). Her purple devil horn headband was slightly askew, making her look less like a fashionable demon and more like a unicorn with poor spatial awareness. Wren glanced down at her own "Team Jacob" sleep shirt and pink devil horns, wondering if their matching accessories made them look more or less suspicious. Though really, what kind of killers wore bat slippers and did skincare?

"Pass the guac," Riley mumbled through her own face mask, making grabby hands at the bowl between them. On the TV screen, Brad and Janet were getting caught in the rain, which prompted Riley to reach for her water gun with the enthusiasm of someone who hadn't committed vehicular manslaughter three hours ago.

"You know," Wren said, dodging a spray of water, "most people's Halloween traditions don't involve both The Rocky Horror Picture Show and actual horror."

"Hey, we're innovators," Riley replied, squirting the TV one more time for good measure. "Breaking new ground in the field of holiday celebrations. Besides, what else were we supposed to do after…" she waggled her eyebrows meaningfully, "…you know."

"After turning my ex into roadkill?" Wren supplied dryly. "Yeah, I can't imagine that scenario comes up in many self-help books."

Riley snorted, then winced as the movement cracked her face mask. "I mean, they should really update those books. Times are changing. People have needs."

"Right?" Wren reached for a chip, carefully navigating around her drying face mask. "Like, there really should be a 'Murder for Dummies' book. Chapter One: So You've Accidentally Killed Someone - Now What? Chapter Two: The Proper Way to Stress Eat After Homicide."

On-screen, Dr. Frank-N-Furter appeared, prompting them both to grab pieces of toast from their carefully prepared pile. They threw them at the TV with perhaps a bit more vigor than necessary, probably working out some residual aggression.

"You know what's weird?" Riley said, reaching for another piece of toast. "This is actually kind of therapeutic. Like, who needs anger management when you can just throw bread at your TV?"

"Pretty sure that's not what our therapists would recommend," Wren replied. "Though I guess it's better than throwing cars at people."

"Too soon?"

"Way too soon."

The criminologist appeared on screen, his neck conspicuously absent as always, and they both yelled, "He's got no fucking neck!" with enough volume to probably wake the neighbors. Though after the night's events, Wren figured disturbing the peace was pretty low on their list of crimes.

"Hey," Riley said suddenly, turning to face Wren with an expression that suggested she'd just had either a brilliant idea or a stroke. "We should get a cat."

Wren blinked, her face mask cracking further. "A cat."

"Yeah! Like, an emotional support animal for

our trauma. Plus, it would make us look more normal. Nobody suspects cat ladies of murder, right?"

"I'm pretty sure that's not actually true," Wren pointed out. "Also, we literally just proved we probably shouldn't be responsible for any living things right now."

"But we'd be great cat moms!" Riley protested. "We're organized, we're good at cleanup, we know how to handle dead things—"

"And there it is."

"I'm just saying, we've got transferable skills!"

Wren reached over and patted Riley's knee. "Sweetie, I love you, but I think we should maybe wait on pet adoption until we've processed the whole 'killing someone' thing. Baby steps."

They fell into silence for a moment, watching as Janet sang about touching herself. The face masks were starting to itch, and Wren could feel a strange heaviness settling in her chest that had nothing to do with the clay mixture.

"You know what's really messed up?" Riley said suddenly, her voice softer than before. "I keep thinking about my vape. Like, I'm more upset about losing that than about…" She gestured vaguely at nothing.

"Than about turning Josh into a human speed bump?"

"Yeah." Riley picked at a loose thread on her pajama pants. "Is that bad? That feels bad."

Wren considered this, absently reaching for more guacamole. "I mean, probably? But also, your vape never tried to control your life or stalk you, so maybe it's justified."

"True. My vape was a better boyfriend than Josh ever was."

"That's both accurate and deeply concerning."

They watched as Frank-N-Furter strutted across the screen in his corset and fishnets. Wren couldn't help but think that if they were going to commit murder, they could have at least done it with better costumes. Scooby-Doo characters seemed a bit basic in retrospect.

"Oh god," Riley said suddenly, sitting up straight. "We still have that Linguistics midterm tomorrow."

Wren burst into a fit of hysterical giggles. "Right, because that's definitely our biggest problem right now. Not the fact that we spent our Halloween playing real-life Grand Theft Auto."

"I'm just saying, Professor Godwin is scarier than any cop."

"Pretty sure the penalty for failing a midterm isn't life in prison."

"No, it's worse," Riley said solemnly. "It's summer school."

They both dissolved into giggles that time, which quickly turned into full-blown laughter that had more than a hint of panic to it. Wren's face mask was definitely ruined now, cracking and flaking onto her shirt like some sort of metaphor for her crumbling sanity.

"We're going to hell," Riley gasped between laughs. "We are absolutely going to hell."

"Bold of you to assume we're not already there,"

Wren replied, wiping tears from her eyes.

The movie continued playing, its familiar scenes providing a bizarre backdrop to their post-murder breakdown. Wren watched as Brad and Janet's world spiraled further into chaos, feeling a strange kinship with their bewilderment. Though at least they only had to deal with a sweet transvestite from Transsexual, Transylvania. Not the moral implications of justifiable homicide.

"Wren?" Riley's voice had taken on that serious tone she usually reserved for discussions about climate change or whether pineapple belonged on pizza.

"Yeah?"

"I think tonight might have fucked us up a little."

Wren looked at her best friend, taking in the smeared face mask, the crooked devil horns, the slight tremor in her hands as she reached for another chip. "Yeah," she said softly. "I think you might be right."

They sat in silence for a moment, the weight of the night's events settling around them like a heavy blanket. Or maybe that was just the emotional exhaustion kicking in. It was hard to tell the difference when you'd spent your evening playing real-life Criminal Minds.

"Well," Riley said finally, reaching for the guacamole bowl, "I guess we'll deal with that when it hits us. Until then, I'm just going to focus on not failing tomorrow's midterm. And maybe investing in a better shovel, because that one we used? Not ergonomic at all."

"Your priorities continue to concern me," Wren replied, but she was smiling. She stood up, stretching until her back cracked. "I'm going to bed. Try not to have any murder-related nightmares."

"Too late for that," Riley called after her as she headed toward her room. "But hey, at least we've got face masks on. Can't have bad dreams if your face is too tight to move, right?"

"Pretty sure that's not how that works."

"Let me have this, Wren. Let me have this."

Wren paused in her doorway, looking back at her best friend. Riley was still sprawled on the couch, the bowl of guacamole balanced precariously on her stomach, The Rocky Horror Picture Show casting flickering shadows across her face mask. She looked ridiculous and vulnerable and exactly like the kind of person you'd want by your side during an accidental homicide.

"Good night, Riley," Wren said softly. "Love you."

"Love you too," Riley replied, not looking away from the TV. "Even if you are Team Jacob."

Wren rolled her eyes and closed her door, the movie's iconic "Don't dream it, be it" echoing through their small house. The irony wasn't lost on her. They'd definitely dreamed up something tonight—a nightmare, specifically. But hey, at least they had good skincare routines to show for it.

She crawled into bed, her bat slippers discarded by the door, and stared at the ceiling. Somewhere in the distance, she could have sworn she heard police sirens, but that might have just been paranoia. Or maybe it was just the universe's way of providing appropriate background music for her inevitable descent into madness.

Either way, she had a midterm to worry about. And really, wasn't that scarier than any murder investigation?

(Spoiler alert: it wasn't. But denial was a hell of a coping mechanism.)

PART TWO

THE GIRLIE POP MURDER CLUB

"You're killing people."
"No, I'm killing boys."
- *Jennifer's Body*

8
WREN

THE FIRST RULE OF MURDER CLUB IS SOMEONE ALREADY BROKE THE FIST RULE OF MURDER CLUB

November 17th, 2014
11:47 P.M.

The fluorescent lights of Riverside State University's library flickered with all the stability of Wren's recent life choices, which was to say: not very. She stared at her Linguistics textbook, the words swimming before her eyes like alphabet soup. Next to her, Riley had completely given up the pretense of studying and was drawing tiny stick figures being eaten by what looked suspiciously like sharks in the margins of her notes.

"That's dark," Wren commented, nodding at Riley's doodles. "Though I guess we're not really in a position to judge anyone's coping mechanisms."

Riley glanced up, the dark circles under her eyes making her look like she'd lost a fight with her eyeliner. "Hey, at least I'm being creative with my trauma. Besides, these aren't sharks." She tapped her pen against the paper. "They're dolphins. Murderous dolphins."

"Well, at least it fits. Dolphins do tend to be more violent than sharks."

The library was almost empty this late, occupied only by the most desperate of students preparing for finals and one very bored-looking student worker who'd been fighting sleep for the past hour. The quiet should have been peaceful, but instead, it felt oppressive, like the silence itself was listening.

Seventeen days. That's how long it had been since Halloween night. Since Josh. Since everything changed. Wren's mind drifted back to the police questioning, which had been about as fun as getting a root canal while simultaneously taking a statistics test.

"When was the last time you saw Joshua Bennet?" they'd asked. Wren had managed to keep her voice steady as she'd told them about running into him at the Halloween party. It wasn't even a lie – she just conveniently left out the part where he'd followed her home, got hit by a car, and ended up as an unwitting addition to the abandoned cemetery's underground community.

The investigation had been all over campus. Missing person posters with Josh's face were plastered on every bulletin board, lamppost, and pizza place window. His smug smile haunted them even in death, which seemed unfairly on-brand for him.

"We should probably head home soon," Riley said, breaking into Wren's thoughts. "My brain is basically pudding at this point, and I'm pretty sure I just wrote 'Silent letters are just consonants in witness protection' in my notes."

"I mean, you're not entirely wrong," Wren replied, but she was already starting to pack up her books. Every noise in the library – a chair scraping, someone coughing, the distant slam of a door – made her shoulders tense. Hyper-vigilance, she'd learned, was exhausting.

They were almost finished gathering their things when someone slid into the empty chair across from them. Wren looked up to find a guy, about their age, watching them with an intensity that made her immediately want to check if she had something on her face. He was wearing a black hoodie, despite the library's sauna-like heating system, with a beanie pulled low over his eyes.

"Hey," he said casually. As if they were all old friends meeting for coffee instead of strangers in an almost-empty library at midnight. "You're in Professor Godwin's Linguistics class, right?"

Wren exchanged a quick glance with Riley. "Yeah," she answered carefully. "Both of us."

"Cool, cool." He nodded, drumming his fingers on the table. "I'm Parker. I've seen you around campus." His eyes flickered between them, settling on Wren. "Must be hard to focus on schoolwork lately. You know, with everything going on."

The way he said it made Wren's stomach drop. There was something in his tone, something knowing, that set off every alarm bell in her head. She felt Riley go still beside her.

"Finals are pretty stressful," Riley said lightly, but Wren could hear the tension underneath.

Parker's lips curved into a small smile. "I wasn't talking about finals." He leaned forward slightly, lowering his voice. "I was talking about Josh Bennet's disappearance. Must be especially hard for you, given your history with him."

Wren's mouth went dry. She'd gotten pretty good at deflecting questions about Josh over the past couple of weeks – from the police, concerned professors, and nosey classmates. Who all suddenly wanted to be her friend now that she was slightly connected to the most exciting thing to happen on campus since someone released three greased pigs in the administration building.

But there was something about Parker's direct gaze that made her usual carefully crafted responses stick in her throat.

"It's been rough," she managed, aiming for appropriately somber but not suspiciously so. The art of appearing just the right amount of upset about your ex-boyfriend's disappearance was something they didn't teach in college. "But we're managing."

"I'm sure you are." Parker's fingers continued their rhythm on the table, like he was playing the silent melody of our demise. "It's interesting though, isn't it? How nobody's found any trace of him. Almost like he just... vanished into thin air." His eyes met Wren's. "Or into the ground."

Riley's hand shot out under the table, grabbing Wren's knee in a grip tight enough to bruise. Wren forced herself to maintain eye contact with Parker, even as her heart threatened to burst out of her like an alien chestburster.

"What exactly are you getting at?" Riley's voice had lost all its usual warmth, dropping into something cold and sharp.

Parker glanced around the library. The student worker had finally succumbed to sleep, their head resting on the desk. The few other students were absorbed in their own studies, earbuds firmly in place. When he looked back at them, his expression was eerily calm.

"I saw you that night," he said quietly. "Halloween. I was walking home from a party when I saw him standing in your walkway. Then I heard the argument, and saw what happened with the Jeep." He shrugged like he was discussing the weather instead of vehicular homicide. "I stuck around long enough to see you drag him into the garage."

The world seemed to tilt sideways. Wren felt like she was going to throw up, possibly all over her Linguistics textbook.

"That's..." Riley started, but Parker cut her off with a raised hand.

"Before you try to deny it, or come up with some

elaborate explanation, let me be clear: I don't care that you killed him." His voice was matter-of-fact, almost bored. "From what I heard that night, and what I know about Josh's reputation, he probably had it coming. What I care about is that you got away with it."

Wren found her voice, though it came out raspy. "Got away with what? We didn't—"

"The police questioned you both, right?" Parker interrupted. "Probably within days of his disappearance. But they didn't look too hard at you, did they? Because who would suspect two college girls? Especially when one of them is the ex-girlfriend – too obvious, right? And the other one..." He nodded at Riley. "Well, you've got that whole golden girl vibe going on. Nobody looks twice at the pretty blonde in the denim jacket."

Riley's grip on Wren's knee tightened. "If you're trying to blackmail us—"

"I'm not." Parker leaned back in his chair, his hoodie falling open slightly to reveal a worn t-shirt underneath. "Like I said, I don't care that you did it. In fact, I think you did the world a favor. What I want is your help."

The silence that followed was heavy enough to crush diamonds. Wren's mind raced through their options. They could deny everything, but Parker seemed pretty confident in what he'd seen. They could try to intimidate him, but that seemed like a bad idea. They could kill him too, but Wren was pretty sure there was a rule about diminishing returns when it came to solving murder with more murder.

"Our help," she repeated slowly. "With what?"

Parker's expression darkened. "My ex. Nik. He's... well, let's just say he makes Josh look like a boy scout. And unlike Josh, he's smart enough to keep his abuse under the radar. No paper trail, no witnesses, nothing that would hold up in court." His fingers stopped their drumming, curling into a fist. "I've tried everything legal. Restraining orders, police reports, even tried to get him kicked out of school. But nothing sticks. He always finds a way around it."

"That sounds terrible," Riley said carefully. "But what exactly do you expect us to do about it?"

"The same thing you did with Josh." Parker's voice was steel. "Make him disappear."

Chapter 3: Phonology. The Sound Pattern of Language

Phonetics provides the means of describing speech sounds; phonology studies the ways in which speech sounds forms systmes and patterns in human language.

phoneme: abstract unit
phone: a phonetic unit and segment

The different phones that represent or are denied from one phoneme are called the allophones

Minimal Pairs: Pairs of words that differ by only one phoneme, proving two sounds are separate phonemes.

Examples: bat vs. pat, cat vs. mat.

Silent letters are just consonants in witness protection

Parker
555-987-5643

9
RiLEY

FUN FACT: MOST STARTUPS DON'T BEGIN WITH BODY COUNTS

12:35 AM

Riley had always thought that if she ever became a criminal mastermind, her lair would be something impressive — maybe an abandoned warehouse with cool mood lighting, or at least a basement that didn't have mold issues. Instead, here she was, planning murder in their rental house's living room, surrounded by empty Red Bull cans and what appeared to be every takeout container from the past month. There was probably a metaphor in there somewhere about the unoriginality of evil, but she was too caffeinated to figure it out.

Parker sat perched on the edge of their secondhand

couch like he thought it might bite him, which wasn't entirely unreasonable given its mysterious stains and questionable structural integrity. The bravado he'd shown in the library had evaporated somewhere between there and here, replaced by the kind of nervous energy usually reserved for first dates or colonoscopies.

"So," Wren said, breaking the awkward silence that had settled over them like a particularly uncomfortable blanket. "Spill the beans."

Parker swallowed hard. "Could I... could I get some water first?"

"Water?" Riley snorted. "Bold of you to assume we have anything that healthy. We've got Red Bull, more Red Bull, and what might be a Pepsi from last semester." She grabbed a can from their fridge, which was essentially a Red Bull storage unit with delusions of grandeur. "Here. Nothing helps you discuss murder plans like heart palpitations."

He accepted the can with trembling hands, and Riley felt her initial suspicion start to soften. It was hard to see him as a threat when he looked like he might pass out at any moment. Plus, his hoodie had a small pride pin on it, which somehow made him seem more trustworthy. Though Riley supposed that was probably faulty logic — being queer didn't automatically make you a good person, just like being straight didn't automatically make you Josh.

"Okay," Wren prompted, settling into their ratty armchair like it was a throne. "Let's hear about this ex of yours."

Parker took a long sip of Red Bull, wincing slightly at the taste. "Right. Nik." His voice caught on the name. "We met last year in Bio lab. He was... charming, at first. Everyone loved him. He had this way of making you feel special, you know? Like you were the only person in the world who mattered."

Riley did know. That was the thing about guys like that – they were always charming at first. It was practically page one of the Abusive Boyfriend Handbook.

"But then things changed," Parker continued, his grip tightening on the can until it started to crinkle. "It was little things at first. He didn't like my friends. Thought they were a bad influence. Then he started checking my phone, showing up at my work unannounced. Said it was because he cared, because he worried about me." He laughed, but there was no humor in it. "By the time I realized what was happening, I was in too deep."

Riley moved to sit next to him on the couch, careful to keep some distance. "And you said you went to the police?"

"Multiple times." Parker's voice was bitter now. "But Nik's smart. He never left marks where people could see them. Never sent threatening texts that could be traced. Always had an alibi. And when I finally got a restraining order?" He shook his head. "He found ways around it. Started showing up at places he knew I'd be, just far enough away to technically not be violating the order. Sent his friends to keep tabs on me."

"What a prince," Wren muttered. "I'm starting to see

why you came to us."

Parker nodded, taking another sip of Red Bull. "Last week, he..." He trailed off, blinking rapidly. "Let's just say he made it clear that restraining orders are just pieces of paper."

Riley felt something cold settle in her chest. She glanced at Wren, saw the same anger reflected in her friend's eyes. They'd killed Josh for being a stalker – this guy sounded way worse.

"Look," Riley started, trying to be rational despite the rage building inside her. "What happened with Josh was... complicated. We got lucky. We don't exactly have a foolproof system for this kind of thing and —"

"We'll do it."

Riley's head snapped up at Wren's words. Parker made a sound somewhere between a gasp and a sob, launching himself at Wren in a hug that nearly knocked over the armchair. Riley watched as her best friend awkwardly patted Parker's back, looking about as comfortable as a squirrel in a dog park.

"Thank you," Parker whispered, his voice thick with tears. "Thank you so much."

"Yeah, well," Wren extracted herself from his grip, straightening her clothes. "Just remember – loose lips sink ships. And in this case, 'ships' means 'our collective freedom and future ability to not wear orange jumpsuits.'"

They spent the next few minutes exchanging contact information, with Wren firmly establishing their "no digital trail" rule. "Seriously," she emphasized, "no texts, no calls, no tweets about your upcoming murder plans. I don't care how good the hashtag would be."

Parker nodded earnestly, clutching his phone like it was a lifeline. "I understand. Complete secrecy." He stood up, looking steadier than he had all night. "I should go. But... thank you. Both of you."

Riley watched him leave, waiting until the front door closed before rounding on Wren. "Have you completely lost your mind? Did killing Josh activate some kind of secret murder gene? Because I'm pretty sure 'serial killer' wasn't on either of our career aptitude tests!"

Wren remained calm, sprawled in her armchair like some kind of alternative lifestyle crime boss. "Think about it, Riley. Josh is gone. He's not out there stalking anyone else, not making any other girl feel unsafe in her own home." She leaned forward. "We could do that again. Help people who have no other options."

"By murdering their exes?"

"By removing threats." Wren's eyes were intense. "Come on, you heard Parker's story. Vik is dangerous, and the system isn't helping. Sometimes bad people need to have very permanent accidents."

Riley collapsed onto the couch, grabbing Parker's abandoned Red Bull and downing it in one go. "I can't believe we're actually considering this. We're going to end up on one of those true crime podcasts. 'The Girlie Pop Murders: Two College Students' Journey from Finals to Felonies.'"

"That's actually not a bad title."

"Not helping!"

Wren grinned, but it faded quickly. "Look, I know it's crazy. But maybe we're exactly the right kind of crazy for this. Nobody suspects us – you said it yourself, we got lucky with Josh. Maybe we can use that luck to do some good."

"Pretty sure 'doing good' and 'committing murder' aren't mutually exclusive."

"Says who? Robin Hood stole from the rich. We just... permanently remove abusive assholes from the dating pool."

Riley stared at her best friend, trying to find a flaw in her twisted logic. The problem was part of her – the part that still remembered the fear in Parker's voice, the part that had felt so satisfied knowing Josh could never hurt Wren again – actually agreed.

"Fine," she sighed, reaching for another Red Bull. "But if we're really doing this, we need a better plan than 'hit them with my car and hope for the best.'"

"Agreed. Though you have to admit, the car thing worked pretty well."

"Yeah, but I don't want that to be my signature move. People will start calling me the Jeep Reaper or something."

Wren snorted. "That's actually kind of badass."

"Still not helping!"

They sat in silence for a moment, the weight of their decision settling around them like a particularly judgmental fog. Finally, Riley spoke up.

"Hey, Wren?"

"Yeah?"

"Do you think this is what they meant by 'girl power'?"

Wren threw a pillow at her head. "Pretty sure the Spice Girls weren't advocating for vigilante justice."

"No, but 'If you wanna be my lover, you gotta not be an abusive asshole' doesn't have the same ring to it."

Wren threw another pillow, this time hitting Riley squarely in the face, but she was laughing. Because really, what else could you do when you'd just agreed to become some sort of discount Dexter meets Charlie's Angels? At least they had plenty of Red Bull to fuel their descent into organized crime.

Though maybe they should invest in some water. Proper hydration seemed important for serial killing.

10
RiLEY

FIVE STARS: SHIRT ARRIVED BEFORE THE BODY WAS FOUND

November 18th-21st, 2014

There seemed to be a million different ways to commit murder, according to Riley's extremely thorough (and probably concerning) Google search history. A million and one, if you counted "hit them with your car," which she definitely did, given their track record. T h e fact that she was currently sprawled on a picnic blanket comparing murder methods like they were spring break destinations probably said something about her mental state, but that was a problem for future Riley and her eventual therapist.

"Your aura is disturbingly cheerful for someone

planning homicide," Wren commented, watching as Riley color-coded her list of potential murder weapons. The remote corner of campus they'd chosen for their planning session was empty except for a few questionably motivated squirrels and Parker, who looked about as comfortable as a vampire at a garlic festival.

"Okay," Wren said, keeping her voice low despite the fact that the nearest person was approximately three zip codes away. "Tell us about Nik's schedule."

Parker picked at the grass nervously. "He works the night shift at the Gas-N-Go on Route 7. Usually gets off around three AM. After his shift..." He hesitated. "He drives out to this spot by the lake. Kind of his personal hideaway, I guess. He goes there to drink and..." Another pause. "Cool down."

Riley didn't like the way Parker's voice caught on those last words. She'd seen enough crime shows to read between the lines. "Cool down from what exactly?"

"From whatever – or whoever – made him angry that night." Parker's fingers were systematically destroying a blade of grass. "He's got a temper. Likes to take it out on things. Or people."

"Charming," Wren muttered. "So he's alone out there? No witnesses?"

"Usually. Sometimes he brings friends, but not often. Mostly he just sits in his car, drinks, and blasts music until sunrise."

Riley exchanged a look with Wren. An isolated location, a predictable schedule, and a habit of getting drunk? It was like Vik was gift-wrapping himself for murder.

"We could make it look like an accident," Wren mused. "A drunk driving incident, maybe?"

"Too obvious," Riley countered. "Everyone knows he goes there to drink."

They spent the next hour tossing around ideas, each one more elaborate than the last. Parker contributed occasional details about Nik's habits, but mostly he just looked increasingly pale, like he was watching a tennis match between two particularly murderous players.

The next day, Riley sprawled on Wren's bed while her best friend paced the room, gesturing with an empty coffee cup like she was conducting a very caffeinated orchestra.

"What if," Wren said, stopping mid-pace, "we spike his drink? Something that would knock him out, make him pass out in his car. Then we could move him to the water, make it look like he stumbled in while drunk."

"Hmm." Riley rolled onto her stomach, considering. "Not bad, but it feels... I don't know, generic? Like we're plagiarizing from every crime show ever." She sat up suddenly. "Oh! What if we sabotage his car?"

Wren raised an eyebrow. "Go on."

"Well, we know he'll be drinking, right? So we mess with his car while he's doing his whole brooding-by-the-lake routine. When he tries to leave, it won't start. He'll get out to check what's wrong, and then…" Riley made a stabbing motion with her hand. "Surprise!"

"Did you just mime murder?"

"I'm a visual learner."

Wren laughed, but her eyes were sparkling with that dangerous light that meant she was getting excited about an idea. "That could actually work. We could inject him with something when he's distracted with the car."

"Exactly!" Riley jumped up, getting into the spirit of their twisted brainstorming session. "And just think of all the one-liners we could use!"

"Oh no."

"Oh yes! Like, 'Looks like your engine's flooded… just like you will be!'"

Wren groaned. "That's terrible."

"How about 'You should've checked your fluids, Vik!'"

"Getting worse."

"'Guess you're running on empty now!'"

"I'm beginning to regret this entire friendship."

Riley flopped back onto the bed, grinning. "Come on, if we're going to be vigilante murderers, we need some good catchphrases. It's like, Serial Killer 101."

"Pretty sure that's not a real course."

"It could be. We could teach it!"

The next day, Riley could barely contain her excitement as she burst into Wren's room, clutching a package to her chest like it contained the secrets of the universe instead of what was actually inside.

"Close your eyes!" she demanded.

Wren, who was trying to study for their Linguistics final, didn't even look up. "The last time you said that, you'd drawn faces on all our soda cans and wanted to introduce me to their 'unique personalities.'"

"This is way better!" Riley insisted. "Come on, humor me."

Wren sighed but closed her eyes. Riley quickly opened the package and pulled out its contents with a flourish. "Okay, open!"

Wren's eyes went wide as she took in the light pink t-shirts Riley was holding up. Each one had "TGPMC" printed across the front in dark pink letters.

"What," Wren said slowly, "the hell is TGPMC?"

Riley beamed. "The Girlie Pop Murder Club! I made us club shirts! I'm the president, and you're the VP, secretary, treasurer, and snack monitor."

There was a moment of silence before Wren burst out laughing. "You made murder club t-shirts? Are you actually insane?"

"Probably!" Riley tossed one of the shirts at her. "But admit it, they're cute."

"They're evidence is what they are."

"They're team building! Besides, no one will know what it means. We could tell people it stands for... uh...

The Great Pumpkin Magic Club!"

"In November?"

"The Gay Pride Music Collective?"

"Better, but still ridiculous."

Riley pulled her shirt on over her tank top, striking a pose. "Fashion doesn't have to make sense, Wren. It just has to look good while we commit felonies."

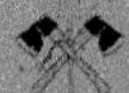

The final planning session took place by the lake, because apparently they were going all-in on the whole "return to the scene of the future crime" aesthetic. Parker had driven them out to scout the location, and Riley had to admit, it was perfect for murder. Isolated, dark, with plenty of places to hide a body – or, in their case, one very specific body.

"So," Riley said, kicking at some loose gravel. "About body disposal. I might have an idea."

Both Wren and Parker turned to look at her expectantly.

"There's this old cistern near here. Found it when I was a kid – scared the hell out of my parents when they caught me trying to use it as a 'secret clubhouse.'" She gestured vaguely toward a barely visible path. "It's deep, covered with this huge rusty lid, and basically forgotten by everyone except tetanus-seeking children and, apparently, murderous college students."

Wren's eyebrows shot up. "How do you just casually

know about perfect body-dumping spots?"

"I was an adventurous child with questionable judgment. Still am, apparently."

They hiked out to check the cistern, which was exactly as creepy and perfect as Riley remembered. The metal lid groaned when they lifted it, revealing a deep, dark hole that seemed purpose-built for hiding evidence.

"Well," Riley said cheerfully, "at least we know where we're dumping the trash."

Wren shot her a look. "You're enjoying this way too much."

"I prefer to think of it as finding silver linings in our descent into organized crime."

They stood there for a moment, looking out over the lake. The water was dark and still, reflecting the cloudy sky above like a mirror. In two days, they'd be back here, not to plan a murder but to commit one. Riley felt a strange mix of emotions – fear, excitement, determination, and a weird urge to make more t-shirts.

"You know," she said thoughtfully, "I feel like we should have some kind of team cheer or something."

"Absolutely not," Wren replied immediately.

"What about a secret handshake?"

"No."

"Team song?"

"Riley."

"Fine," Riley sighed dramatically. "But I'm still wearing my club shirt under my murder outfit. For luck."

Parker, who had been quiet for most of their

planning, suddenly spoke up. "You guys are really weird, you know that?"

Riley grinned, throwing an arm around his shoulders. "Welcome to The Girlie Pop Murder Club, Parker. We may be weird, but at least we're effectively weird."

As they walked back to the car, Riley couldn't help but feel a sense of anticipation building. In forty-eight hours, they'd be back here with a very different purpose. It should have scared her more, this casual planning of murder, but somehow it felt right. Like they were balancing some cosmic scale, one abusive ex at a time.

Plus, she'd already ordered more t-shirts in different colors. Because if you're going to start a murder club, you might as well look fabulous doing it.

★★★★★

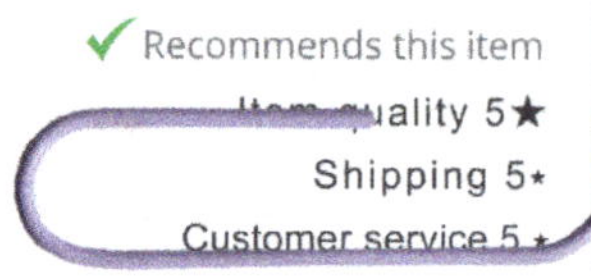

OBSESSED with these custom shirts!! Perfect for our totally legal late-night club activities

The sizing runs true (unlike my alibi lmao jk jk). The pink is giving major femme fatale energy, which is exactly the vibe I was going for when planning our next club meeting by the lake

The vinyl lettering is super high quality - hasn't cracked or peeled even after some pretty intense physical activity (nothing suspicious I promise). Had to order more because the first one got some unexpected stains that definitely weren't suspicious and were totally just Red Bull I swear.

The shop owner asked zero questions about what TGPMC stands for, which we love in a small business! Customer service was killer (pun intended but also please don't flag this review).

Shipping was faster than my Jeep, which is saying something if you know what I mean (you don't, and that's probably for the best).

Only complaint is that they don't come in black (harder to see stains just saying), but the pink actually works better for our aesthetic. We're going for more of a "who, us? 🙄" vibe anyway.

Will definitely be ordering more as our club expands! (FBI if you're reading this it's just a book club I swear)

P.S. Does anyone know if these are washing machine safe or should I just burn them after u... I mean... just kidding!

Helpful? | Report Review

Purchased item: Custom T-Shirts-- FAST SHIPPING!

 RILEY NOVEMBER 27, 2014

11
WREN

WHEN YOUR BACKUP PLAN IS JUST 'BE HOT AND MURDER HIM'

November 23rd, 2014
2:00 AM

Murder, Wren decided, had a very specific smell. Like anxiety and Red Bull and the lingering scent of whatever discount body spray Parker had apparently bathed in before their rendezvous. She wrinkled her nose as she double-checked their supplies in the dim light of Riley's phone: duct tape, gloves, towels, and a backup sedative that they'd probably end up accidentally stabbing themselves with because their lives were just that kind of cosmic joke.

"Everyone remember the safe word?" Riley

whispered as they gathered their gear. At Wren's pointed look, she added, "What? Even murderers need good communication skills."

"The safe word is 'shut up before someone hears us,'" Wren muttered, shouldering their bag of definitely-not-suspicious supplies. They'd parked the Jeep a mile from the lake, which meant hiking through woods in the middle of the night like the world's most amateur horror movie victims.

Parker tripped over a root for the third time in as many minutes. "I didn't realize murder involved so much cardio," he wheezed.

"Right?!" Riley agreed. "Between Josh and this, we're basically getting our PE credits in homicide."

"Pretty sure that's not how credits work," Wren said, but she was fighting a smile. Leave it to Riley to turn murder into an academic achievement.

The November air bit through their black clothing – because of course they'd dressed like cartoon burglars, complete with Riley's insistence on wearing her TGPMC shirt underneath "for luck." Wren's breath came out in little clouds as they trekked through the woods, making her feel like a very unsuccessful dragon.

Finally, they spotted Nik's car, a beat-up Honda that was probably compensating for something. Music blasted from inside – was that actually Kid Rock? Wren's moral compass might be permanently damaged, but even she knew that was a crime worthy of punishment.

"Okay," she whispered, crouching down behind a

bush. "Remember the plan. I'll disable the car, you two stay hidden until I give the signal."

Wren crept toward the Honda, staying low and moving as quietly as possible. The music from inside was loud enough to cover any small sounds she might make – and seriously, who voluntarily subjected themselves to this much Kid Rock? She reached the driver's side and pulled out the small tool kit they'd brought, her hands shaking slightly as she tried to remember everything she'd learned from their late-night YouTube binge of "How to disable a car."

The hood release was easy enough to find, but as she reached up to pop it, her elbow knocked against the side mirror. She froze, but nothing happened. With renewed confidence, she lifted the hood as gently as possible, wincing at the small creak it made. The engine compartment was a maze of parts that definitely hadn't looked this complicated in the YouTube videos.

"Okay," she muttered to herself, "just need to find the…" She reached in, trying to locate the right wire to cut. Her hand brushed against something, then something else, and suddenly—

The car alarm went off with a shriek that probably woke up half the county.

"Well," Riley muttered from her hiding spot, "there goes our element of surprise."

Before Wren could respond, Vik stumbled out of his car, looking exactly like the kind of guy who would listen to sad boomer rock alone by a lake at 2 AM. His eyes were glazed from whatever he'd been drinking, but they focused on Wren with surprising sharpness.

"What the fuck?" he slurred, taking a step toward her. "What are you doing to my car?"

Wren's mind raced. The original plan was clearly shot, which meant improvising. And because her brain was apparently determined to make questionable decisions, she did the first thing that came to mind.

She giggled. Not just any giggle – a full-on ditzy sorority girl giggle. "Oh my god, is this your car? I'm so sorry!" She straightened up, letting her voice go high and breathy. "My friend and I were just walking by and saw someone cute sitting out here alone…"

Nik's expression shifted from anger to interest faster than his car could go from zero to sixty. "Yeah?" He tried to lean casually against his car but missed slightly. "Just couldn't resist, huh?"

"You caught us," Wren laughed, then called out, "Riley! Come on out, he's not mad!"

Riley emerged from the bushes looking like she was trying very hard not to commit murder right then and there. Which, technically, she was.

"We were thinking," Wren continued, stepping closer to Nik, "since it's such a nice night… maybe we could go swimming?"

"Swimming?" Nik's eyebrows shot up. "It's fucking freezing."

"Skinny dipping," Wren clarified, and watched his brain short-circuit.

Riley made a choking sound that she quickly turned into a girlish laugh. "Come on," she coaxed, clearly catching on to Wren's plan. "Live a little."

Nik didn't need much more convincing. He was stripping off his clothes before Wren could even pretend to start removing hers, revealing a body that definitely didn't justify his ego.

"Ladies first," he called as he waded into the water, his voice hitting that specific pitch of masculine entitlement that made Wren want to drown him even more than she already did.

Oh, wait. That was actually the plan.

"What are we doing?" Riley hissed as they pretended to undress, keeping their clothes on under the cover of darkness.

"Improvising," Wren whispered back. "He's drunk, we're two against one, and drowning looks like an accident."

"This is why you're the brains of this operation."

They waded into the water, which was approximately the temperature of Satan's freezer. Wren's teeth chattered as they swam toward Nik, who was making increasingly crude comments about body heat and sharing it.

"Hey," he called out, "you girls still got your clothes on?"

"Just shy," Wren called back sweetly, then gave Riley a quick nod.

They lunged simultaneously, catching Nik mid-lewdness and forcing him under the water. He came up spluttering, panic replacing the sleazy confidence in his eyes.

"What the f—" was all he managed before they pushed him down again.

The struggle was nothing like the movies. It was messy and desperate, with Nik's hands clawing at them as he fought to surface. His fingers found Riley's wrist at one point, squeezing hard enough to make her yelp, but Wren twisted him away, using her weight to keep him under.

Finally, after what felt like hours but was probably only minutes, he stopped moving.

They backed away, treading water and staring at the dark shape floating face-down in the lake. The only sound was their heavy breathing and the distant echo of Kid Rock still playing from Nik's car because apparently, even death couldn't escape bad music choices.

"Holy shit," Riley gasped as they stumbled onto shore, their wet clothes clinging to them like particularly judgmental second skins. "Holy shit holy shit holy—"

"Guys?" Parker emerged from his hiding spot, looking pale even in the darkness. "Is he…?"

"Very," Wren confirmed, wringing water out of her hair. Her hands were shaking, though whether from cold or adrenaline, she couldn't tell. "Now we need to make sure we didn't leave anything behind."

They worked quickly, gathering their supplies and wiping down any surfaces they might have touched. Parker kept glancing nervously at the lake like he expected Nik to rise from the water like some kind of fratboy Kraken.

The walk back to the Jeep was silent, broken only by their squelching footsteps and Riley's occasional muttered "holy shit." It wasn't until they were safely inside the car, heater blasting, that Riley spoke properly.

"Well," she said, pulling her vape from the glove compartment, "at least I didn't lose this one this time."

Wren started laughing, a slightly hysterical sound that would have sent any therapist running for their prescription pad. "That's what you're focusing on? Not the fact that we just drowned someone?"

"I'm choosing to celebrate the small victories," Riley declared, taking a long pull from her vape. "Like not losing my stuff during murder. Personal growth, you know?"

"You're both insane," Parker said from the backseat, but he was smiling slightly.

"Says the guy who asked us to kill someone," Wren pointed out.

"Fair point."

They drove home in comfortable silence, the radio playing softly in the background. As they pulled into their driveway, Riley suddenly sat up straight.

"Oh my god," she said, turning to Wren with wide eyes. "We totally missed the opportunity to say 'sleep with the fishes' when we drowned him."

Wren reached over and flicked her forehead. "You're the worst vigilante ever."

"Yeah, but I'm your vigilante."

"Unfortunately true."

They climbed out of the Jeep, their clothes finally

starting to dry into uncomfortable stiffness. Parker headed off toward his dorm with a quiet thank you and a promise to keep in touch, leaving Wren and Riley standing in their driveway at 4 AM, fresh from their second murder.

"So," Riley said as they walked inside, "does this mean we're officially a club now? Because I ordered more t-shirts in different colors."

12
WREN

HOW TO WRITE MURDER CLUB BYLAWS

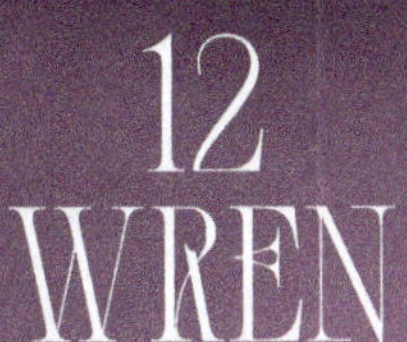

November 26th, 2014
8:15 P.M.

Three days after drowning Vik, Wren found herself sprawled on their threadbare couch, eating cold pizza and contemplating the ethics of starting a murder-based extracurricular activity. The adrenaline had worn off, replaced by a strange emptiness that felt suspiciously like the aftermath of finals week – exhausted, slightly traumatized, but with an odd sense of accomplishment.

"You know what's weird?" Riley said from her position on the floor, where she was surrounded by what looked like a small shrine made entirely of Red Bull cans.

"The second murder was actually easier than the first."

"Pretty sure that's not something to brag about," Wren replied, but she knew what Riley meant. With Josh, they'd been panicked, sloppy. But Vik? That had been almost… professional. The fact that this thought didn't terrify her probably should have.

"Do you think we're becoming sociopaths?" Riley asked, arranging her Red Bull cans into what appeared to be a scale model of Stonehenge. "Like, is this our villain origin story?"

"Pretty sure sociopaths don't worry about becoming sociopaths." Wren paused. "Though I guess that's exactly what a sociopath would say."

Riley sat up suddenly, knocking over her caffeine monument. "Oh! Speaking of organized crime – look what came in the mail!" She jumped up and ran to her room, returning with a familiar package. "The rest of the shirts arrived!"

"The rest of the shirts?" Wren raised an eyebrow. "How many murder club t-shirts does one actually need?"

"Well, we have the original pink ones, but I also got black for night operations, navy for casual murder days, and purple because it's your aesthetic." Riley pulled them out one by one, displaying them with all the enthusiasm of a reformed cheerleader who'd found her true calling in homicide.

"TGPMC," Wren read aloud, running her fingers over the letters. "The Girlie Pop Murder Club. You know, when I joined a sorority, this wasn't exactly what I had in mind."

"Please, we're way more exclusive than any sorority. Our initiation ritual is literally murder."

Wren snorted, but then grew serious. "If we're really doing this – and I can't believe I'm saying this – we need rules. We need to turn our murder club into a properly regulated organization, because apparently, that's where my life is heading."

"Ooh, yes!" Riley grabbed a notebook and pen. "Murder Club Charter, Rule Number One…"

"No digital communication about club business," Wren said firmly. "No texts, no emails, no tweets about your homicidal achievements."

"But think of the hashtag potential!"

"Think of the prison potential."

Riley sighed dramatically but wrote it down. "Fine. Rule Two?"

"Only target people who deserve it," Wren said. "We're not running a general murder service here. This is strictly for taking out the trash."

"Like a very permanent recycling program."

"Riley."

"What? I'm just saying, we're basically ecological terrorists. Removing toxic waste from the environment."

Wren threw a pizza crust at her. "Rule Three: Always have an alibi. We need to be somewhere else every time something happens."

"Oh! We could join a book club!" Riley's eyes lit up. "The perfect cover – we'll be discussing murder mysteries while actually committing murders. It's like inception, but with homicide."

"That's… actually not a terrible idea." Wren shook her head. "Rule Four: All evidence gets destroyed. Completely. No souvenirs."

"Does that include the t-shirts?"

"The t-shirts aren't evidence if no one knows what TGPMC means."

"See? This is why you're the brains of the operation." Riley scribbled in her notebook. "Rule Five?"

"Never talk about the club to outsiders." Wren paused. "Except Parker, I guess, since he's technically our first client."

"Client makes it sound so professional." Riley tapped her pen against her chin. "Like we're running a small business. Murder & Associates: Your Problems Are Our Solutions."

"Your business plan needs work."

They spent the next hour refining their rules, adding sub-clauses and exceptions because even vigilante justice required proper paperwork. Riley insisted on adding "Must wear official club merchandise during operations" as a rule, which Wren vetoed on the grounds of "literally everything about that is a terrible idea."

"We should probably be more careful about choosing targets in the future," Wren said, grabbing the last slice of pizza. "Parker was different — we knew the situation was bad. But we can't just help anyone who asks."

"Agreed. We need like, a vetting process. References.

Maybe a Yelp review system?"

"'Five stars, would recommend for all your murder needs'?"

"Exactly!"

Riley jumped up suddenly, disappearing into the kitchen and returning with a bottle of cheap champagne they'd been saving for… well, probably not for this specific occasion, but it seemed fitting.

"To the official founding of The Girlie Pop Murder Club," Riley declared, wielding the champagne bottle like she was christening a very questionable ship. "May our aim be true and our alibis unbreakable."

"To being really, really good at murder," Wren added, accepting a plastic cup of slightly warm champagne. "Which is definitely not a phrase I ever expected to say."

They clinked their cups together, settling back into the couch. The TV droned in the background – some true crime show that now felt less like entertainment and more like a how-not-to guide.

"Hey," Riley said after a while, her voice casual in a way that immediately made Wren suspicious. "So, hypothetically, if I told you I've been keeping a list of potential future targets…"

Wren turned to look at her best friend, taking in the mixture of enthusiasm and uncertainty on her face. "Let me guess – you've got files on them already?"

"Maybe a small spreadsheet."

"Color-coded?"

"Obviously. What kind of amateur murderer do you

think I am?"

Wren laughed, shaking her head. "We'll cross that bridge when we come to it. For now, let's just focus on not getting caught for the murders we've already committed."

"Speaking of which," Riley said, reaching for the champagne bottle, "we should probably add a rule about proper hydration during murder. Lake water is not a suitable substitute for H2O."

"That's… oddly specific yet practical."

"I contain multitudes." Riley raised her cup again. "To murder with good skincare!"

"To questionable life choices!"

"To The Girlie Pop Murder Club!"

Their laughter echoed through the small house, two college girls celebrating their new extracurricular activity with all the enthusiasm of newly declared majors. The fact that their major was murder was just a minor detail, really. Besides, every club needed a niche, and they'd found theirs – it just happened to involve more homicide than the average student organization.

At least their t-shirts were cute.

PART THREE

YAAS, QUEEN!
SLAY!!

"Look, I know killing people is wrong. But this is like... good
murder."
- Sheila Hammond *Santa Clarita Diet*

13
RiLEY

MURDER LLC: WE PUT THE SLAY IN SLAYING IT

November 28, 2014 – December 12, 2014

Word of mouth marketing is way trickier when the "mouth" part could land you in prison. Riley sat cross-legged on their living room floor, surrounded by a fortress of empty Red Bull cans and the entire snack inventory of the campus vending machines, trying to figure out how to advertise services you definitely couldn't post on LinkedIn.

"What about business cards?" she suggested, earning an eye roll from Wren, who was sprawled on their couch with a notebook filled with what looked suspiciously like murder logistics. "No, hear me out – we could make them really cute. Pink and glittery, with little skulls in the corners."

"Right," Wren drawled, not looking up from her notes. "Because nothing says 'discreet murder service' like announcing our crimes in holographic cardstock."

"Well, we need some way to let people know we're open for business," Riley argued, her hands automatically building another Red Bull can tower like a caffeinated game of Jenga. "We can't exactly put up flyers: 'Got an abusive ex? We've got an ax!'"

Parker, who was perched on their armchair like someone who'd recently discovered it was actually a mimic, cleared his throat. "I could… help with that. You know, spread the word to people who might need your services. Carefully, of course."

Riley brightened. "Like a murder matchmaker!"

"More like a highly selective referral service," Wren corrected, finally looking up from her notebook. "We'd need strict criteria. No random revenge seekers or people with petty grudges. Only cases where traditional justice has failed and the target poses a genuine threat."

"So basically, we're like a really extreme version of Yelp," Riley mused. "Instead of one-star reviews, we just remove the whole restaurant."

Wren threw a pillow at her head. "We need to stay anonymous. No one except Parker can know who we are. Which means…" She trailed off, her eyes lighting up with the kind of spark that usually preceded either a brilliant plan or their imminent arrest. "We need disguises."

Twenty minutes later, Riley found herself staring at

their reflection in the bathroom mirror, contemplating whether this was rock bottom or just a particularly creative pit stop on the way there. They were wearing matching leopard print cat masks that covered the top half of their faces, complete with little ears and painted-on whiskers. The masks had been left over from some forgotten Halloween costume attempt, discovered in the depths of their closet along with what appeared to be the graveyard of abandoned Pinterest projects and at least one suspicious sock puppet.

"We look like we're about to rob a Claire's," Riley observed, adjusting her mask. "Or start the world's most fashionable crime syndicate."

"That's kind of the point," Wren replied, fixing her whiskers with surprising precision for someone planning multiple homicides. "No one's going to take two girls in cat masks seriously, which means no one's going to look too closely at us."

"Josie and the Pussycats Go Psycho," Riley quipped. "I dig it."

Their chosen meeting spot for clients was equally ridiculous – an abandoned fire escape that led down to what could generously be called an underground bunker beneath one of the older campus buildings. The space had probably been designed for storage or emergency shelter, but now it mainly housed cobwebs, mysterious puddles, and what Riley hoped was just a very large rat (she'd named it Maurice and already ordered him a tiny TGPMC shirt).

"It's perfect," Wren declared as they set up shop in their underground lair. "No cameras, multiple escape routes, and hardly anyone knows it exists."

"Plus," Riley added, "if anyone does find us down here, we can just pretend we're filming a really low-budget superhero movie. 'The Adventures of Murder Cat and Her Sidekick, Slightly More Murderous Cat.'"

They established a system: potential clients would leave cash and target details in a designated spot, and if the case met their criteria, they'd arrange a meeting through Parker. It felt like running a start-up, if start-ups specialized in permanent customer removal. Riley even caught herself mentally drafting elevator pitches: "We're disrupting the revenge industry with our innovative approach to problem elimination."

Wren developed her own ritual, memorizing the names of their targets like she was studying for a particularly morbid final exam. Riley would sometimes catch her muttering them under her breath, reciting them like a hit list disguised as a grocery list: "Josh, Vik, and counting..."

Their first new target was Greg, a serial abuser who had somehow managed to avoid any legal consequences despite multiple restraining orders. They cornered him in an alley, Wren wielding an ax with the energy of someone who'd found her true calling in hardware store weapons.

"You know," Riley whispered as they waited in the shadows, "We really should have some kind of catchphrase for these moments. Like 'Your time's up!' or 'Justice is served!'"

"How about 'you're going to get us caught and we'll be the ones who end up murdered'?" Wren suggested sweetly.

When Greg walked past, distracted by his phone, Wren struck with surprising efficiency. As they dragged his body into deeper shadows, Riley couldn't help but comment, "I guess you could say he got the ax."

"I'm going to murder you next."

"That's the spirit!"

Dylan was next – a stalker who had terrorized multiple women on campus. They lured him to the lake with a fake drug deal (apparently their reputation for murder hadn't affected their ability to seem like potential customers, which Riley found mildly concerning).

The woodchipper had been Parker's idea, though Riley suspected he'd been joking when he suggested it. Still, there was something oddly satisfying about watching Dylan become fish food.

"Look on the bright side," Riley said as they cleaned up. "He's finally contributing to the ecosystem. Circle of life and all that."

"Pretty sure this isn't what The Lion King meant," Wren replied, but she was fighting a smile.

Blythe's "hunting accident" was probably their most elaborate setup yet. They'd spent days planning the perfect spot, making sure it would look like a tragic suicide rather than murder. As they watched him fall, Riley couldn't help but appreciate the poetry of using his own hobby against him.

"I guess his hunting days are over," she quipped as they rolled his body into the cistern.

"Do you have a pun for every murder?"

"I'm building my repertoire. Think of it as professional development."

The murders started blending together after that, each one adding to their growing reputation in certain circles. Tyler's car accident ("Guess his brakes needed checking!"), Nathan's climbing mishap ("Talk about a steep learning curve"), Michael's protein shake surprise ("Should've read the ingredients list"), Peter's rooftop swan dive ("Hope he enjoyed the view!"), Jacob's cabin explosion ("Some like it hot"), Zach's nightclub exit ("Last call came early"), and Nick's parking lot farewell ("He should've carpooled").

Through it all, Wren kept her mental list, each name a notch in their belt of vigilante justice. Riley watched her friend sometimes, wondering if they should be more concerned about how easily this had become their new normal. But then she'd remember why they were doing this — remember Josh's stalking, Nik's abuse, all the others who had hurt people without consequence — and the doubt would fade.

They ended most nights in their underground meeting spot, counting cash and reviewing potential cases like they were running a particularly murderous student council. Riley had even started keeping minutes, though she had to get creative with the euphemisms: "Monthly goals: Reduce local toxicity levels. Team building exercise:

Synchronized waste removal. Budget concerns: Need more cleaning supplies."

"You know what we should do?" Riley said one night, sprawled on their makeshift desk (a door perched on old milk crates that had probably witnessed more crimes than most detectives). "Start a rewards program. Like, every fifth murder is free."

Wren looked up from her notebook, where she was probably calculating optimal body disposal routes or planning their eventual prison break. "We're not a coffee shop, Riley."

"No, but we could be! 'The Daily Grind: Where Every Shot is a Kill Shot.' It's called diversifying our business model."

"I'm starting to think the Red Bull has rotted your brain."

"Bold of you to assume I had brain cells to spare."

They sat in comfortable silence for a while, the weight of their actions settling around them like a particularly judgmental security blanket. Through the small window near the ceiling, Riley could see stars peeking through the November sky, twinkling innocently above their underground chamber of vigilante justice.

"Hey, Wren?"

"Yeah?"

"Do you think we should be more worried about how good we're getting at this?"

Wren was quiet for a moment, her fingers tracing the names in her notebook. "Probably," she said finally. "But then again, we probably should have been worried way back when you hit Josh with your car."

"Fair point." Riley stretched, her cat mask slightly askew. "At least we look cute while committing felonies."

"That's definitely going on our tombstones: 'They died as they lived – fashionably murderous.'"

"Speaking of fashion," Riley sat up suddenly, "I've been thinking about expanding our merchandise line. How do you feel about murder club hoodies?"

The pillow that hit her face was probably deserved, but Riley maintained that her business ideas were solid. After all, what was a secret murder club without branded merchandise? It was just good business sense, really.

Even if their target demographic was literally dying to get in.

Riley's to-do list:
1. Gaslight (the police)
2. Gatekeep (murder secrets)
3. Girlboss (order more club t-shirts)
4. Maybe commit some murder (if time permits)

14
WARREN

THINGS DETECTIVES DON'T EXPECT: GLITTER AT CRIME SCENES

December 15, 2014
9:15 AM

*D*etective William Warren had forgotten how the morning fog in Riverside Hollow wrapped around everything like a possessive lover's embrace. He pulled his black sedan into the police station parking lot, the leather of his steering wheel creaking under his grip as he took in the familiar brick building. Twenty years away, and the place still looked exactly the same – right down to the crooked satellite dish that had probably been transmitting static since his high school graduation.

The dashboard clock blinked 9:15 AM, but it felt

earlier. Maybe it was the fog, or maybe it was the weight of twelve bodies that had brought him back to his hometown. A dozen deaths and disappearances in just over a month wasn't just unusual for Riverside Hollow – it was like someone had decided to turn their quiet college town into a true crime podcast.

Bill stepped out of his car, his worn leather shoes crunching on gravel that had witnessed two decades of small-town secrets. The air smelled like wet leaves and wood smoke, with an underlying hint of whatever culinary war crime the campus cafeteria was attempting to pass off as breakfast. Some things never changed.

The station's front desk was staffed by Betty Marshall, who looked exactly like she had when Bill was sneaking cigarettes behind the gymnasium twenty years ago – right down to the look that could make hardened criminals confess just to escape her judgment. She glanced up as he entered, and her expression shifted from professional distance to surprised recognition.

"Well, if it isn't Billy Warren," she said, her voice carrying enough small-town memory to fill a yearbook. "Finally decided to grace us with your big-city presence?"

"Betty," he nodded, managing a small smile. "Still keeping this place running, I see."

"Someone has to." She jerked her thumb toward the chief's office. "He's expecting you. Though I hope you realize your return is going to keep the gossip mill running longer than the backup generator."

"Glad to contribute to the local entertainment

economy."

Chief David Porter's office looked like a filing cabinet had declared war on organization and won. The man himself sat behind his desk, his mustache exactly as bushy as Bill remembered, though now it looked like it had been seasoned with two decades of small-town politics.

"Warren," Porter greeted him, gesturing to a chair that had probably heard more confessions than the local church. "Thanks for coming back. Didn't really want to handle this one in-house."

Bill settled into the chair, which creaked ominously. "Twelve deaths in a month will do that. What've you got?"

Porter handed over a thick file labeled "Case 27B57" in neat block letters. "Started with a missing persons case right after Halloween. Josh Bennet, local college student. Ex-girlfriend reported him missing after he didn't show up for classes for a few days."

"The ex reported it?" Bill's eyebrows rose slightly as he flipped open the file. "That's unusual."

"Yeah, well, that's not the only unusual thing about this case." Porter leaned back in his chair. "After Bennet disappeared, it's like the town decided to audition for Final Destination. We've got drownings, car accidents, a hunting mishap, a woodchipper incident – hell, someone even managed to fall off a mountain."

Bill's eyes scanned the list of names, his instincts humming like a tuning fork set to suspicion. "Any connections between the victims?"

"Other than them all being grade-A assholes?" Porter

shrugged. "Most had some history of domestic issues, harassment complaints, that sort of thing. Nothing that stuck in court, but enough to make their obituaries read like public services."

"So someone's cleaning house," Bill murmured, more to himself than Porter. His finger traced down the list: Josh Bennet, Victor "Vik" Martinez, Greg Thomas, Dylan Cooper… each name either followed by a date of disappearance or cause of death, each "accident" more creative than the last.

"If they are, they're doing a damn good job of making it look accidental." Porter's mustache twitched. "Medical examiner's only flagged a couple as suspicious, but the sheer number in such a short time…" He trailed off, letting the implications pile up like bodies.

Bill lingered on Josh Bennet's file. Twenty-two years old, business major, multiple complaints filed against him for stalking and harassment, like a résumé written in red flags. His ex-girlfriend, Wren Martinez, had taken out a restraining order just two weeks before his disappearance. Last seen at a Halloween party, presumably heading home.

"The ex-girlfriend," Bill said slowly. "What's her story?"

Porter shuffled through some papers. "Wren Martinez. Senior at Riverside State. Lives off-campus with her roommate, Riley Thompson. Both good students, no criminal records. Martinez filed the restraining order against Bennet after he started showing up at her workplace, sending threatening messages, the usual stalker playbook."

"And Thompson? The roommate?"

"Seems clean. Though she did drive the same model Jeep that was spotted near Bennet's last known location." Porter held up a hand as Bill's expression sharpened. "Already checked it out. She was at a Halloween party all night, multiple witnesses."

Bill nodded, but something about it nagged at him. He'd learned long ago to trust his instincts, and right now they were telling him that this was more than just a string of unfortunate accidents. Someone was orchestrating these deaths, and they were smart enough to make them look random.

"I'll start with Martinez," he decided, standing up. The chair gave one final protest before falling silent. "If there's a connection here, it probably starts with Bennet."

Porter nodded. "Just remember, this isn't like your big city cases. People talk here. If word gets out that we're treating these as suspicious deaths…"

"The whole town will know before lunch," Bill finished. "Don't worry, I remember how it works here."

He left the station with the file tucked under his arm, his mind already mapping out possible angles. The fog had started to lift, revealing a town that seemed almost too peaceful for the darkness lurking beneath its surface.

As he drove toward the outskirts where Martinez lived, Bill couldn't shake the feeling that he was missing something obvious. Twelve deaths, each one carefully staged to look accidental. Someone was playing a very dangerous game, and they were good at it – maybe too good.

His rearview mirror caught the "Welcome to Riverside Hollow" sign, its cheerful paint at odds with the growing body count. Below it, someone had spray-painted "Where Dreams Come True!" in neon pink letters.

"More like where nightmares come true," Bill muttered, turning onto the street where Wren Martinez lived. Time to find out if the ex-girlfriend knew more than she was letting on.

After all, revenge was as good a motive as any. And in his experience, the most dangerous predators were the ones who looked like prey.

15
WREN

HOW TO NOT LOOK SUSPICIOUS
(A PINTEREST GUIDE)

10:23 AM

The thing about murder, Wren was discovering, was that it really wreaked havoc on your ability to enjoy simple domestic tasks. Here she was, trying to organize her art supplies like a normal person who definitely hadn't helped dispose of multiple bodies, when the knock at the door made her nearly impale herself on a particularly sharp paintbrush.

She froze, paintbrush still clutched like a weapon, and crept toward the door. Through the peephole, she could see a man in his thirties wearing the kind of casual blazer that screamed "I have authority but I'm trying to seem approachable." Her breath caught slightly as she took in his appearance - tall and broad-shouldered, with dark hair just starting to silver at the temples in a way that was frustratingly attractive. Great. Because that's exactly what she needed on a Monday morning – an unexpectedly handsome authority figure.

"Miss Martinez?" His voice carried through the door with practiced ease. "I'm Detective Bill Warren. I was hoping to ask you a few questions about some recent incidents around campus."

Wren's eyes darted to the cat masks lying on the coffee table – their super-secret murder club disguises that suddenly seemed about as subtle as a neon sign advertising "DEFINITELY NOT MURDERERS HERE." She kicked them under the couch just as she opened the door, plastering on her best "I'm just a normal college student who definitely hasn't started a murder-based extracurricular activity" smile.

"Detective Warren," she said, stepping aside to let him in. "What kind of incidents?"

He entered with the careful observation of someone who was probably cataloging every detail of their living room, from the stack of true crime books on the coffee table (maybe not their best decoration choice) to the half-finished art projects scattered around (turns out murder was great for creative inspiration). Wren found herself suddenly very aware of the paint smudges on her hands as his intelligent grey eyes swept the room. He moved with the kind of easy confidence that probably came from years of making people nervous in their own homes, though that didn't fully explain why her pulse had picked up slightly.

"Just following up on some missing persons cases," he said, settling into their armchair like he owned it. The morning light from their window caught the silver in his hair, and Wren had to actively remind herself that appreciating how it complemented his sharp jawline was probably not the appropriate response to being questioned about multiple murders. "Including Josh Bennet. I understand you two had a history?"

"If by history you mean he couldn't take no for an answer," Wren replied, perching on the edge of the couch. "We dated briefly, it ended badly, and then he decided stalking was an acceptable hobby."

Warren's expression remained neutral, but his eyes were sharp. "And the night he disappeared? Halloween?"

"I was at a party," Wren said, the lie flowing easily after weeks of practice. "Left early because Josh showed up and started causing problems. Went home, watched Rocky Horror Picture Show, did face masks. You can check my Instagram – I'm pretty sure I posted about it."

"Interesting night for self-care," Warren commented mildly.

"Well, having your stalker ex show up at a party kind of kills the mood. Sometimes you just need to throw toast at your TV and pretend the world doesn't suck."

He started listing other names – Vik, Greg, Dylan – watching her face carefully for any reaction. Wren maintained her confused expression, though internally she was reciting her list of victims like a particularly morbid mantra.

"Should I know these people?" she asked, tilting her head. "I mean, I've heard about some disappearances on campus, but it's a big school."

"Big school, small town," Warren countered. "Mind if I take a look around?"

Wren's heart did a complicated gymnastics routine, but her voice stayed steady. "Actually, I do mind. No offense, but I'm not really comfortable letting strange men wander through my house without a warrant. Even ones with badges."

"Just trying to be thorough."

"And I'm just trying not to end up as a cautionary tale about letting strange men into my bedroom. You want to search the place? Come back with a warrant."

The front door opened then, and Riley walked in, her usual bouncy entrance faltering at the sight of their unexpected guest. She was wearing one of their TGPMC shirts under her jacket, because apparently the universe had decided today was "Let's Make Wren Have a Heart Attack" day.

"Um, hi?" Riley said, looking between Wren and Warren with poorly concealed concern.

"Detective Warren was just asking about Josh," Wren explained, putting slight emphasis on the name to warn Riley. "And some other missing students."

"Oh," Riley said, dropping onto the couch next

to Wren. "That's still going on? I figured he just, like, transferred schools or something."

Warren turned his attention to Riley, and Wren could practically see him noting her nervous energy. She watched as he shifted forward slightly, his grey eyes focusing with an intensity that really shouldn't have been as compelling as it was, especially given the circumstances. "Miss Thompson, right? You drive a Jeep Grand Cherokee?"

"Yeah?" Riley's confusion wasn't entirely fake – they hadn't expected anyone to connect those dots. "Lots of people drive Jeeps. They're great for... Jeep things."

"Jeep things," Warren repeated slowly.

"You know, like... driving. And... more driving."

Wren jumped in before Riley could dig that hole any deeper. "We were both at the Halloween party when Josh disappeared. Riley was designated driver, which is why she remembers the night so clearly."

"Super clearly," Riley agreed quickly. "Totally remember being completely sober and definitely not hitting anyone with my car."

Wren fought the urge to facepalm. Sometimes she wondered how they'd gotten away with multiple murders when Riley had all the subtlety of a drunk giraffe in a tutu.

Warren's eyes narrowed slightly, but his expression remained friendly. "Well, ladies, thank you for your time. If you think of anything else..." He handed Wren his card. "Give me a call."

The moment the door closed behind him, Riley collapsed dramatically onto the couch. "Oh my god, that was terrifying. Did you see how he looked at us? Like he could see right through our souls! Also, do you think he noticed my shirt? Because I just realized what I'm wearing and I'm having a minor panic attack."

"Riley," Wren said slowly, "what part of 'be subtle' translates to 'definitely not hitting anyone with my car'?"

"I panic-ramble! You know this about me!" Riley sat up suddenly. "Wait, how did he know about my Jeep? And why is he asking questions now? It's been over a month!"

Wren was already grabbing Riley's laptop. "Let's find out exactly who we're dealing with."

Ten minutes of intensive Googling revealed several unsettling facts about Detective Bill Warren:

- He had a 95% solve rate for cold cases
- He specialized in uncovering serial killers
- He had grown up in Riverside Hollow
- He was known for being particularly persistent when he sensed something was off

"Well," Riley said, reading over Wren's shoulder, "we're totally screwed."

"Not helping."

"I'm just saying, maybe we should consider a career change. Something less murder-adjacent. Like professional cat herding or underwater basket weaving."

Wren paced the living room, her mind racing. They'd been careful — maybe not at first, but they'd gotten better at covering their tracks. But if Warren was as good as his reputation suggested...

"We need to be extra careful," she decided. "No

more clients for a while. And we should probably move our meeting spot, just in case."

"What about the cat masks?"

"What about them?"

"Well, if he comes back with a warrant, do we just say we're really into furry fashion?"

Wren stopped pacing to stare at her best friend. "Sometimes I worry about what goes on in your head."

"Hey, I'm just trying to think of plausible explanations for our murder accessories!" Riley protested. "Though I guess 'fashion statement' is better than 'murder club uniform.'"

They spent the next hour doing damage control – hiding anything suspicious, reviewing their alibis, and trying to figure out how much Warren might already know. The weight of his suspicion hung over them like a particularly judgmental cloud.

"You know what the worst part is?" Riley said finally, sprawled on the floor surrounded by their hastily gathered murder supplies. "I saw you checking him out, and I totally get it. He's got that whole sexy detective vibe going on."

"Please don't develop a crush on the man trying to arrest us for multiple homicides." Though Wren had to admit, if someone was going to end their murder spree, at least it was someone who looked like he'd walked out of a crime drama.

"I'm just saying, if we weren't murderers and he wasn't trying to catch us, it could be a meet-cute!"

"Riley."

"What? I contain multitudes! I can appreciate both murder and murder-solving!"

Wren couldn't help but laugh, even as anxiety churned in her stomach. That was the thing about Riley – she could always find humor in the darkness, even when that darkness was wearing a detective's badge and asking very specific questions about their Halloween activities.

Still, as she watched Riley attempting to organize their "definitely not murder-related" supplies into neat piles, Wren couldn't shake the feeling that Warren's visit was just the beginning. He seemed like the kind of detective who could smell secrets, and they had enough of those to fill a particularly disturbing memoir.

"Hey," Riley said suddenly, holding up one of their cat masks. "If we do get caught, can we at least make sure our mug shots are fabulous? I want to be trending on Twitter for something other than murder."

Sometimes Wren wondered if they should be more concerned about how well they were adjusting to life as serial killers. But then again, what was the point of vigilante justice if you couldn't look good doing it?

Even if "looking good" currently involved leopard print cat masks and a very persistent detective on their trail.

Evidence
January 13, 2015
Case Number 27b57
Detective: W.W.

The Girlie Pop Murder Club

Murder? I Barely Know Her! (But We'll Kill Him For You)

Riley Thompson

PRESIDENT

Phone
1-800-YASS-DIE
(1-800-927-7343)

Email
TGPMC@icloud.com

No Body, No Problem! Ask About Our Holiday Specials!

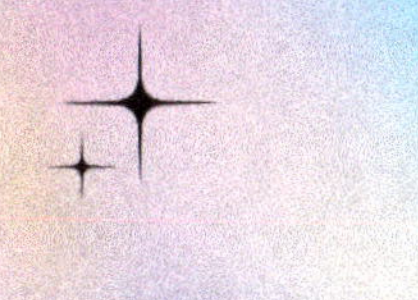

TGPMC: Because Therapy is Expensive but Murder is Free! ✨ (Terms and conditions apply. No refunds. All sales are final. Like, really final.)

16
WREN

DOES THIS MURDER EVIDENCE SPARK JOY?

December 18, 2014
3:45 PM

Wren hadn't slept properly in three days. Not since Detective Warren's visit had turned their cozy murder club into what felt like an episode of Criminal Minds, except they were definitely not the good guys. She'd spent countless hours replaying their conversation in her head. Analyzing every word like she was trying to decode ancient prophecies instead of casual lies about face masks and Rocky Horror Picture Show.

"You know," Riley said from her position on the floor surrounded by what looked like every cleaning supply they owned, "I'm pretty sure if you keep stress-cleaning that spot, you're going to wear a hole through to the neighbor's apartment."

Wren looked down at the counter she'd been scrubbing for the past twenty minutes. "I just want to make sure we haven't missed anything. DNA, fingerprints—"

"The meaning of life?" Riley suggested. "Because at this point, you might find it under all that bleach."

"This isn't funny, Riley. Warren isn't some small-town cop we can easily fool. He specializes in serial killers."

"Which we technically aren't," Riley pointed out. "We're more like... selective population control specialists. With a very specific target demographic."

Wren threw her sponge at Riley's head. "Focus! We need to do a complete sweep of the house. Anything that could connect us to the murders needs to go."

They started in the living room, which looked like a crime scene in reverse – instead of collecting evidence, they were desperately trying to eliminate it. Riley kept up a running commentary as they worked, because apparently impending arrest made her even more talkative than usual.

"You know," she said, stuffing their cat masks into a garbage bag, "we could just burn the place down. Start fresh somewhere else. Maybe open a cute little café where we definitely don't murder anyone."

"Pretty sure arson would just add to our growing list of felonies."

"True, but at least it would be festive. Nothing says 'holiday spirit' like deliberately setting fires."

They found the axe they'd used on Greg hidden behind their winter coats, which seemed like a terrible storage choice in retrospect. Various disguises were stuffed in the back of closets, and there was an alarming number of suspicious stains that needed addressing.

"We've gotten sloppy," Wren muttered, scrubbing at a particularly stubborn mark on their bathroom floor that she really hoped was just hair dye. "We need better alibis for all the nights in question."

Riley perked up. "Oh! I can get Sarah from my Bio class to say we were at that bar crawl the night Greg disappeared. She was so drunk she barely remembers her own name, let alone who was actually there."

"Perfect. And I can probably convince Jake that I was at his party when Dylan went missing." Wren grabbed her phone, starting to scroll through old photos. "We should backdate some social media posts too. Make it look like we were nowhere near any of the crime scenes."

"Already on it," Riley said, tapping away at her phone. "Just posted a throwback photo of us at that coffee shop downtown. Tagged it from the night of the woodchipper incident. You know, when we definitely weren't turning Dylan into fish food."

"Could you maybe not phrase it like that?"

"Sorry. When we were definitely not engaging in aquatic ecosystem enhancement?"

Parker showed up around sunset, looking appropriately nervous for someone who'd helped establish a murder-based business model. He settled onto their newly sanitized couch like he thought it might be bugged, which, given their current paranoia levels, wasn't entirely unreasonable.

"Has anyone been talking?" Wren asked, cutting straight to the point. "Any whispers about what we do?"

Parker shook his head. "Nothing specific. Some people are connecting the dots about abusive guys going missing, but no one's linked it back to us."

"They better not," Wren said, her voice dropping to something dangerous. "Because if anyone starts talking, we all go down. And I don't think you want to find out how creative we can get with problem-solving."

"Was that a death threat?" Riley whispered loudly. "Because it sounded super badass."

Parker just nodded, probably wondering how he'd ended up involved with two girls who discussed murder with the same casualness most people reserved for brunch plans.

After he left, Riley dove back into her Detective Warren research, which had become increasingly concerning. "Did you know he once solved a cold case by noticing the brand of coffee someone drank?" she said, scrolling through news articles. "Like, who pays attention to coffee brands? Should we switch coffee brands? Is our coffee incriminating?"

"I think we have bigger problems than our coffee preferences," Wren replied, but she made a mental note to maybe switch to a different brand anyway. Just in case.

"Oh god," Riley said suddenly, her face illuminated

by her laptop screen. "His sister was killed by her abusive boyfriend twenty years ago. The guy got away with it – insufficient evidence or something. That's why he's so invested in cases like this."

Wren felt her stomach drop. "He's not going to let this go, is he?"

"Not likely. But hey, at least we know why he's so determined. Silver linings?"

They were interrupted by a knock at the door that nearly gave them both heart attacks. It turned out to be just their elderly neighbor, Mrs. Henderson, asking if they'd seen her cat. But the surge of adrenaline was enough to remind them how precarious their situation had become.

"We need an exit strategy," Wren said later that night, pacing their freshly cleaned living room. "Somewhere to go if things get too hot."

Riley looked up from where she was making a list of potential hideout locations, which so far included "that abandoned cabin by the lake" and "literally anywhere that isn't prison."

"I have some cash saved up," she offered. "And my aunt has that house in Vermont she never uses. Though I guess murder fugitives probably shouldn't hide out with family."

"Probably not." Wren collapsed onto the couch, suddenly exhausted. "How did we get here, Riley? When did we go from accidentally killing your stalker ex to planning escape routes?"

"Technically, it wasn't an accident. I very deliberately hit him with my car."

"Not helping."

"Sorry." Riley set aside her list and joined Wren on the couch. "But hey, at least we look cute while planning our potential life on the run, right? And I bet we'd rock those orange jumpsuits if it came to that."

Wren couldn't help but laugh, even as anxiety churned in her stomach.

"You know what the worst part is?" Riley said suddenly. "I don't even regret it. Any of it. Does that make us terrible people?"

Wren thought about Josh, about Nik, about all the others who had hurt people without consequence. "Maybe," she said finally. "But maybe the world needs some terrible people to balance out all the other terrible people."

"That's deep," Riley nodded. "Also possibly concerning from a psychological standpoint, but mostly deep."

They sat in silence for a while, surrounded by the evidence of their paranoid cleaning spree. The house smelled like bleach and anxiety, with a hint of the lavender air freshener Riley had insisted on using because "if we're going to be murderers, we might as well have a signature scent."

"Wren?"

"Yeah?"

"If we do have to run... can we at least make it

somewhere with good coffee? Since we apparently have to change our current brand for suspicious reasons?"

Wren threw a pillow at her, but she was smiling. Because really, what else could you do when your best friend was worried about coffee options while planning a potential life as a fugitive?

At least they'd cleaned up all the evidence. Probably. Mostly.

God, they really needed to sleep.

ROCK BOTTOM
(AND OTHER PLACES WE'VE BEEN)

December 19, 2014
11:30 A.M.
Last Day of the Semester

Riley had always thought Linguistics was the most boring class in existence, but apparently, she'd underestimated just how mind-numbing it could be when you were also juggling murder club responsibilities and an increasingly persistent detective.

The fact that it was their last class this semester somehow made it even worse – like the professor was determined to cram an entire semester's worth of morphemes and phonemes into their already overtaxed brains.

She was halfway through drawing tiny stick figures doing increasingly violent things to her textbook (a fitting tribute to her current mental state) when a flash of familiar blonde hair caught her attention.

Megan slipped into class late, keeping her head down, but not before Riley caught sight of the purple-black bruise blooming around her eye. The sight hit Riley like a punch to the gut – or maybe more like a hit from a car, which she had some experience with, thanks to Josh.

The next forty-five minutes were torture. Riley couldn't focus on anything except the way Megan winced every time she moved, the split in her lip that definitely hadn't been there a few days ago, and the careful way she held herself like everything hurt. By the time class ended Riley had mentally planned at least seventeen different ways to murder whoever was responsible, each more creative than the last.

"Megan!" She caught up to her friend in the hallway, trying to keep her voice casual even as rage burned in her chest. "Wait up!"

Megan turned, and Riley's anger flared hotter at the closer view of her injuries. "Hey, Riley. I was actually just—"

"Who did this?" Riley cut her off, keeping her voice low. "And don't say you fell or walked into a door or whatever bullshit excuse you've prepared, because I swear to god—"

"It's nothing," Megan insisted, but her voice trembled

slightly. "Really, I just—"

"Megan." Riley pulled her into an empty classroom, shutting the door. "I'm your friend, and I'm telling you right now that if you don't tell me who did this, I will personally interrogate everyone on campus until I find out. And trust me, my interrogation techniques are… creative."

Maybe it was the steel in Riley's voice, or maybe Megan just needed to tell someone, but she broke down. "It's Scott," she whispered, tears spilling over. "My boyfriend. He… he gets angry sometimes. Says things. Does things."

Riley's hands clenched into fists. "How long?"

"A few months? It wasn't always this bad. He'd just grab my arm too hard or throw things near me. But last night…" Megan's voice cracked. "He said if I told anyone, he'd…"

"I'm going to kill him," Riley said, with the kind of calm certainty usually reserved for discussing the weather or what to have for lunch.

Megan gave a watery laugh. "Don't joke about that."

"Who's joking?" Riley muttered, but she plastered on a reassuring smile. "Just… stay somewhere else tonight, okay? Promise me."

"What do you mean?" Megan asked, sniffing as she narrowed her eyes with suspicion.

"Trust me, it's better that you don't know. If you are ready to get away from this asshat then just… make sure to be somewhere else." Riley gave Megan a soft squeeze on the arm as she spoke, looking into her eyes and making sure she understood what she wasn't saying.

Twenty minutes later, she burst into their rental house with all the subtlety of a hammer to the face (another murder method she'd considered for Scott during her walk home).

"We have a new target," she announced to Wren, who was doing what appeared to be murder-related origami at their kitchen table. (It was different from a regular origami crane in that she'd made it out of their old murder plans, which seemed fitting – turning evidence into art, one fold at a time. Plus, she'd added little angry eyebrows and splattered them with red ink because if you're going to make murder-themed origami, you might as well commit to the aesthetic.) "And before you say no—"

"No," Wren said immediately, because of course she did.

"You didn't let me finish!"

"Let me guess – you want to add another name to our ever-growing list of victims while Detective Warren is actively investigating us? While we're basically one suspicious coffee purchase away from being arrested?"

Riley blinked. "Okay, yes, but when you say it like that, it sounds bad."

"That's because it is bad!" Wren threw up her hands, sending paper cranes flying. "We're already walking a tightrope over a pit of 'going to jail forever,' and you want to juggle while we're at it?"

"It's Megan," Riley said quietly and watched Wren's

expression shift. "That jerk Scott's been hitting her. And before you start listing all the reasons we shouldn't – which, valid, probably – just know that if we don't do something, the next time I see her, it might be in a hospital. Or worse."

Wren was quiet for a long moment, absently folding and unfolding one of her murder cranes.

"We'll need to be careful," she said finally. "Like, professionally paranoid levels of careful."

"So… our normal Tuesday?"

They planned everything meticulously, down to the smallest detail. No more messy car accidents or elaborate setups. This had to be clean, quick, and untraceable. They chose a night when Megan would be staying with her sister, got a copy of Scott's key (amazing what people will do with a sob story and fifty bucks), and gathered their supplies.

"Chloroform?" Riley read off their shopping list. "Isn't that a little… theatrical?"

"Says the girl who wanted to dress up as ninjas for this."

"Hey, if we're going to commit murder, we might as well commit to the aesthetic."

Breaking into Scott's apartment was surprisingly easy, though Riley had to fight the urge to trash the place when she saw the hole he'd punched in his bedroom wall. The bastard was passed out in bed, probably drunk judging by the empty bottles scattered around.

"Sweet dreams, asshole," Wren muttered, pressing the chloroform-soaked cloth over his face while Riley kept watch. Except Scott apparently didn't get the memo about being an obliging victim — he thrashed awake, arms flailing like a caffeinated octopus, nearly knocking Wren off balance.

"A little help here?" Wren hissed, struggling to maintain her grip. "He's not exactly following the movie script!"

Riley dove in, practically body-slamming across Scott's legs while trying to pin his arms. "So much for the peaceful solution," she grunted, catching an elbow to the ribs. "You know, this would be so much easier if chloroform worked like it does on TV. Filing a complaint with Hollywood when we're done."

It took both of them, a lot of awkward wrestling, and what felt like an eternity before Scott finally went limp. They stayed frozen for a moment, half-expecting him to jump up again like some kind of domestic abuse jack-in-the-box.

"Well," Riley panted, rubbing her bruised ribs, "that was fun. Next time, let's just stick to hitting them in the face with hammers. Way less upper body strength required."

They worked quickly, binding him with duct tape and wrapping him in a sheet. Riley had suggested using their cat masks for old times' sake, but Wren had vetoed that with the kind of look that suggested she was reconsidering their entire friendship.

"Plus," she had said, "we tossed those when we cleaned everything up, remember?"

"Yeah, about that. I may have dug them back out," Riley admitted sheepishly.

Wren's glare could have burned a hole through solid steel.

"What? You know how sentimental I am!"

The drive to the lake was tense, filled with Riley's nervous chatter because apparently impending murder made her even more talkative than usual.

"You know what's weird?" she said as they awkwardly carried Scott toward the cistern. "This is kind of like a really dark team-building exercise. Like, instead of trust falls, we have trust murders."

"Riley."

"I'm just saying, we should get credit for this. Like, extra credit for extracurricular activities."

"Please stop talking."

They were almost at the cistern when Scott stirred. Riley felt him twitch and opened her mouth to warn Wren, but it was too late – he burst out of the sheet like the world's worst birthday surprise, knocking Wren to the ground.

What followed was possibly the most awkward fight scene in murder history. Scott, still woozy from the chloroform, stumbled around like a drunk giraffe while Riley grabbed the nearest weapon she could find — a rock that was definitely going to feature in her nightmares later.

"Hey, Scott!" she called, channeling her inner action hero. "Looks like you're about to hit rock bottom!"

The rock connected with his head with a satisfying crack, and he went down hard. Riley didn't hesitate before bringing it down again, making sure he stayed down this time. The morbid reality of the situation might have disturbed someone else, but she simply shrugged it off.

"Really?" Wren said as she picked herself up. "'Rock bottom'?"

"Listen, it's hard to think of good one-liners in the heat of the moment."

They dumped Scott's body in the cistern, both taking extra time to ensure he was actually dead this time. No more surprise wake-ups — they'd had enough plot twists for one night.

Back at home, they sat in exhausted silence, the adrenaline crash hitting them hard. Riley's hands wouldn't stop shaking, and Wren had stress-cleaned the kitchen three times.

"That was close," Wren said finally. "Too close."

"Yeah," Riley agreed. "Next time we should definitely spring for better chloroform. Maybe check Yelp reviews first."

Her phone buzzed with a text from Megan: "Thanks for listening today. You're a good friend."

Riley stared at the message, feeling something dark and satisfied curl in her chest. "No problem," she typed back. "Just looking out for you."

Meanwhile, across town, Detective Warren sat in his car at the far end of Oak Street, just barely able to make out the outline of the girls' rental house in the distance. He'd been there for hours, watching the street through a pair of binoculars and adding notes to his growing file. When headlights finally appeared around 3 AM, he straightened slightly, noting the time in his notebook. Too far away to see details, but close enough to know that two figures had just arrived home at an unusually late hour.

"Girls that age," he muttered to himself, tapping his pen against the steering wheel, "should be out partying or studying for finals. Not taking mysterious midnight drives." He added another note to his file, then settled back to wait. Sometimes the best detective work was just watching and waiting.

Back at the house, Wren was stress-pacing by their front window, peering out at the street for the fifth time in as many minutes.

"That car's been there all night," she said, her voice tight. "The black sedan at the end of the street. I swear it wasn't there yesterday."

Riley, who was sprawled on the couch trying to get dried mud off her favorite murder shoes, looked up. "Maybe it's just someone having a really long booty call? Or studying in their car because their roommate's annoying? Or—"

"Or maybe it's a certain detective who specializes in catching killers?"

"Well, when you say it like that, you make it sound suspicious." Riley tossed her shoe aside. "But hey, at least we know he's dedicated. Most guys would've given up and gone home by now. You have to admire his commitment to the craft."

"This isn't funny, Riley."

"No, but neither is domestic violence, so I'd say we're even." Riley stood up, pulling Wren away from the window. "Besides, if he is watching us, standing here looking suspicious probably isn't helping our 'totally innocent college students' image."

They spent the rest of the night planning their next moves, trying to stay one step ahead of a detective who seemed determined to solve their particular brand of vigilante justice. But even as anxiety churned in her stomach, Riley couldn't bring herself to regret tonight's murder.

After all, some rocks just needed to meet some hard places. Or in this case, some hard heads.

"You know," she said thoughtfully as they finally headed to bed, the strange car still lurking at the end of their street, "maybe we should send Detective Warren a fruit basket or something. Like, 'Thanks for the dedicated surveillance, sorry we're making your job so hard.'"

"I'm going to smother you with a pillow."

"Ooh, add that to our list of murder methods! See? I can multitask – planning our next kill while being stalked by law enforcement. I deserve extra credit for time management."

She really needed to work on her murder puns. And maybe invest in some better curtains.

WAL★MART
ALWAYS LOW

WE SELL FOR LESS
MANAGER RANDALL MUMMERT
(717) 691 - 3150
ST# 1886 OP# 00 667 TE# 67 TR# 06397
CHLOROFORM 002724263727   13.75
GUMMY BEAR 008467219354   4.50
            SUBTOTAL   18.25
     TAX 1 6.000 %   1.09
             TOTAL   19.34
         VISA TEND   80.00

ACCOUNT #6819
APPROVAL #500847
TRANS ID -0176212555234417
VALIDATION -LD9S
PAYMENT SERVICE - E
              CHANGE DUE   60.66

ITEMS SOLD 2

TC# 0707 5398 7222 2814 097

Find a phone plan that meets your
needs at the WM Connection Center
   10/19/14   11:25:39

CUSTOMER COPY

18
RiLEY

TWAS THE NIGHT BEFORE SEARCH WARRANTS

December 20-24, 2014

"You know what's weird?" Riley said, sprawled upside down on their couch like gravity had personally offended her. "We're better at murder than we are at covering up murder. Like, we've got the killing part down to an art form, but the aftermath is still kind of… chaotic."

Wren, who had been pacing their living room for the past hour like she was trying to wear a trench to China, stopped to give Riley her patented "why are we friends" look. "Could you maybe not announce our murder efficiency ratings out loud while there's literally a detective watching our house?"

"Sorry," Riley flipped right-side up, immediately regretting the head rush. "But seriously, we need a plan. Something to throw Warren off our scent. Like… what if we made it look like all our victims were secretly part of an underground fight club?"

"That's literally the plot of Fight Club."

"Okay, but what about—"

"We're also not framing the Illuminati."

"You're no fun." Riley pouted, then brightened. "Oh! What if we made it look like they were all involved in some shady drug stuff? Like, maybe Scott owed money to the wrong people?"

Wren stopped pacing. "That… might actually work. Drug deals gone wrong, debts unpaid – it's messy enough to be believable."

"Plus," Riley added, "it would explain why some of them disappeared and some of them turned up dead. Drug gangs are all about sending messages, right?"

"Have you been watching Breaking Bad again?"

"…maybe."

Their first stop was Parker's place because apparently when you needed sketchy supplies for your fake drug scene, your friendly neighborhood murder middleman was the guy to ask. He opened his door looking like he'd rather be anywhere else, which was fair given their track record of showing up with increasingly concerning requests.

"Let me get this straight," he said after they

explained their plan. "You want me to help you frame a fake drug gang for all the murders you two committed, just so you can throw off the detective who's definitely going to notice that none of this makes sense?"

"When you say it like that, it sounds bad," Riley admitted.

"That's because it is bad!"

But he helped them anyway, probably because Wren had perfected her "help us or join our body count" smile. They left with a burner phone from Parker, while Riley contributed their own stash of weed ("A worthy sacrifice for the cause," she'd said solemnly). Wren pulled out the small stack of worn bills they'd collected as donations from their "clients" — it wasn't much, just enough to usually cover supplies and post-murder snacks, but it would work for their purposes.

"You know what's kind of sad?" Riley said as they drove away. "We're technically the world's worst-paid hitmen. We barely break even after buying cleanup supplies and Red Bull."

"Pretty sure most hitmen don't expense their snacks," Wren pointed out.

"Well, maybe they should. Murder really works up an appetite. We could revolutionize the whole industry — add dental plans, snack budgets, maybe even a 401(k)."

"Please stop trying to turn our murder club into a legitimate business model."

The warehouse they'd picked was perfect — abandoned, creepy, and exactly the kind of place where shady deals definitely went down. Or at least, Riley assumed they did. Her knowledge of drug operations was mainly based on Netflix originals and that one time she accidentally bought oregano thinking it was weed in freshman year.

They worked quickly, setting up their fake crime scene like they were decorating for a very illegal house party. Riley scattered the money around while Wren planted the burner phone, which contained some very dramatic texts about deals and debts (mostly copied from crime shows, but they were hoping the police wouldn't recognize their pop culture plagiarism).

"Should we add some blood?" Riley asked, holding up a bottle of fake blood left over from Halloween. "Make it extra dramatic?"

"Put that away before you—"

Too late. Riley had already knocked over their carefully placed ledger, sending it straight into a puddle. The ink ran like mascara at a breakup, turning their meticulously forged document into abstract art.

"Oops?"

"I swear to god, Riley—"

But before Wren could finish that thought (which, given her expression, was probably going to involve creative uses for the fake blood), voices drifted in from outside. They froze, looking at each other with matching expressions of panic.

"Dude, I swear I saw something in there!"

"You're just high, man."

"No, like, actual people!"

They grabbed their supplies and booked it out the back exit, trying to look casual while speed-walking away from a crime scene. Which, really, they should be better at by now given their extracurricular activities.

The next few days were torture. Riley kept checking news sites obsessively, while Wren stress-cleaned their apartment so thoroughly that even their dust bunnies probably had PTSD.

Finally, on December 23rd, the news broke: "LOCAL POLICE INVESTIGATE POSSIBLE GANG CONNECTIONS IN RECENT DISAPPEARANCES." The article mentioned finding evidence of drug activity and unpaid debts, suggesting the missing men might have gotten involved with the wrong crowd.

"We did it!" Riley cheered, doing a victory dance that looked more like a seizure. "We're criminal geniuses!"

"Don't celebrate yet," Wren warned, but she was smiling slightly. "We still need to be careful. Especially since Warren's probably not buying it."

She was right. At that very moment, Detective Warren was sitting at his desk, frowning at their planted evidence like it had personally insulted his mother. Something about it felt off — too neat, too convenient. And when he ran a background check on Parker, whose fingerprints they'd found on some of the items, things got interesting.

Parker called them later that day, panic evident in his voice. "The police want to question me," he said, sounding like he was one strong breeze away from a breakdown. "What do I do?"

"First, breathe," Wren instructed. "Second, remember what we talked about. You know nothing, you've seen nothing, and you definitely haven't been helping two college girls run a murder-based revenge service."

"Right. Nothing. I know nothing. I am Jon Snow."

"Maybe leave out the Game of Thrones references during questioning," Riley suggested.

They spent the next day destroying anything that could connect them to the warehouse scene. Riley made a game of it, humming the Mission Impossible theme while they burned evidence in their bathroom sink.

"You know," she said, watching their gloves turn to ash, "we should really invest in a proper evidence destruction system. Like a tiny incinerator. We could call it the Evidence-B-Gone 3000."

"We are not buying murder cleanup equipment for Christmas."

Speaking of Christmas – December 24th arrived with a blanket of fresh snow and a desperate need for normalcy. They decided to do Christmas Eve right, complete with holiday movies, cookie baking, and enough hot chocolate to put them into a sugar coma.

"These cookies look kind of serial killer-ish," Riley observed, examining their attempts at festive shapes.

"Like, this snowman definitely looks like he's plotting murder."

"Takes one to know one," Wren replied, but she was smiling as she added red icing that looked disturbingly like blood spatter.

They settled on the couch with their murder cookies and hot chocolate, sharing a huge blanket while The Santa Clause played in the background. Riley had gotten Wren a set of fancy art supplies and a book on "Creative Ways to Dispose of Evidence" (which was actually about composting, but the title felt appropriate). Wren had gotten Riley a new vape (to replace the one buried with Josh) and a shirt that said "Looking Sus" in glitter letters.

"This is nice," Riley said softly, watching Tim Allen fall off a roof for the millionth time. "You know when we're not actively committing felonies."

"We should probably cut back on that," Wren agreed. "The felonies, not the Christmas movies."

"New Year's resolution: commit fewer murders?"

"Maybe start with 'don't get caught for the murders we've already committed.'"

They were just starting Home Alone (which hit differently now that they had experience with creative violence) when the knock came. Three sharp raps that seemed to echo through their cozy Christmas Eve setup like gunshots.

Riley and Wren froze, matching expressions of panic crossing their faces. Through the window, they could see Warren's black sedan parked across the street, barely visible through the falling snow.

"What that what I think it was?" Riley whispered.

Another knock, more insistent this time.

Wren stood up slowly, like too sudden of a movement might spook the door. "Stay there," she said quietly. "And hide the murder cookies."

PART FOUR

GET IN LOSER, WE'RE
GOING FUGITIVE

"What can't we face if we're together?
What's in this place that we can't weather?
There's nothing we can't face.
Except for bunnies."
- I've Got a Theory Buffy the Vampire Slayer

19
WREN

 JINGLE BELLS, PRISON CELLS

December 24, 2014
8:30 PM

The thing about having a detective show up at your door on Christmas Eve was that it really put a damper on the holiday spirit. Wren stared through the peephole at Detective Warren's imposing figure, flanked by several uniformed officers who definitely weren't there to sing carols. Behind her, their half-decorated Christmas tree twinkled mockingly, like it was enjoying the irony of their situation.

The plastic reindeer they'd hung earlier watched the scene with judgmental glass eyes, and Wren could swear the angel on top was giving her a particularly disapproving look. Even their holiday decorations had developed a moral compass, which seemed deeply unfair considering the circumstances.

"It's him," Wren muttered to Riley, who sat on the couch with eyes wide enough to put does to shame. "And he brought friends. Because apparently Secret Santa wasn't exciting enough." She glanced at their pile of wrapped presents under the tree, wondering if "caught by the police" counted as coal-worthy behavior in Santa's book.

Riley's eyes widened further, a feat Wren thought impossible. "Maybe if we're very quiet, they'll think we're not—"

Another knock, more insistent this time, cut through her whispered suggestion. Wren took a deep breath, straightening her Christmas sweater like armor. The reindeer on it smiled back at her with unsettling cheer, completely ignorant of the fact that it was about to witness a very tense confrontation. The bell on its collar jingled mockingly as she moved, and she made a mental note to never again let Riley convince her to buy matching holiday sweaters with actual working accessories. Nothing said "totally innocent" quite like jingling while under police investigation.

"Miss Martinez," Warren's voice carried through the door. "Open up. We have a warrant."

Wren shot Riley a look that clearly said 'hide anything murdery' before opening the door with practiced casualness. She'd gotten surprisingly good at this particular expression - a perfect blend of mild annoyance and innocent confusion, like someone who'd just had their Hallmark movie marathon interrupted.

"Detective Warren," she said, channeling her best 'definitely not a serial killer' smile. "What a festive surprise."

Warren held up the warrant like it was a winning lottery ticket. "We're here to search the premises for evidence related to Greg Thomas's murder. Specifically, the axe used in the killing."

"Wow," Riley piped up from behind Wren. "And here we thought you'd just stopped by for some Christmas cookies. Though I guess an axe murderer would be more of a Halloween thing, right?" She gestured to the plate of cookies on the coffee table.

Wren resisted the urge to facepalm. Sometimes she wondered how they'd gotten away with multiple murders when Riley had all the subtlety of a marching band in a library.

The officers spread through their house like particularly determined termites, opening drawers and checking closets with methodical precision. One of them picked up a framed photo of Wren and Riley at last year's Halloween party, dressed as angels of all things. The irony was not lost on Wren. Warren lingered in the living room, his eyes scanning everything with the kind of attention usually reserved for art galleries or really complicated Where's Waldo puzzles.

"Nice tree," he commented, nodding toward their

half-decorated disaster. "Though that snowman ornament looks a bit… aggressive." His gaze lingered on the candy cane wielding snowman, which Riley had somehow managed to hang at an angle that made it look like it was preparing for combat.

"It's avant-garde," Wren replied smoothly. "You know, commentary on the commercialization of Christmas and all that." She resisted adding that it was also commentary on their recent life choices, which had definitely taken a turn toward the avant-garde themselves.

His eyes met hers, and something electric passed between them—definitely not the kind of spark you wanted with someone trying to arrest you for multiple homicides. Wren blamed it on the eggnog she'd been drinking earlier. Or maybe the stress of hiding murder weapons was finally getting to her.

One of the officers made his way toward the storage area, and Wren's heart did a complicated gymnastics routine. The axe was hidden under a loose floorboard that Riley had rigged after what she called her "DIY murder cleanup phase." The officer's boots squeaked against the hardwood with each step, a sound that seemed to sync perfectly with Wren's rising anxiety. She made a mental note to add "invest in carpeting" to their list of future home improvements, right after "stop collecting murder weapons." The officer's foot pressed down, and the board creaked ominously.

"Hey," Riley suddenly announced, loud enough to wake the dead (which, given their track record, was a concerningly real possibility). "Anyone want hot chocolate? I make a killer version. Wait, maybe I should rephrase that." She was already moving toward the kitchen, nearly knocking over their modest collection of holiday cards - all from people who had no idea their friendly neighborhood college students had developed such specific extracurricular activities.

The officer moved on, and Wren mentally added 'Riley's terrible timing occasionally being perfect' to her list of Christmas miracles. Right up there with 'successfully hiding an axe from law enforcement' and 'managing to keep their TGPMC t-shirts out of sight during a police search.'"

The search continued with excruciating thoroughness. One officer inspected their coat closet, pushing aside their matching devil-horned hoodies with suspicious care. Another rifled through their DVD collection, pausing briefly at their well-worn copy of Dexter - perhaps not the best choice of entertainment given their current situation. Wren made a mental note to invest in more innocuous viewing material. Maybe some rom-coms. Nothing said "not a murderer" quite like a collection of Hugh Grant movies.

As the search wound down with nothing to show for it, Warren approached them again. His presence seemed to fill the room, making Wren uncomfortably aware of how tall he was, and how his grey eyes seemed to see right through her carefully constructed facade. The Christmas lights cast shadows across his face, highlighting cheekbones that really had no business being that attractive on someone actively trying to arrest her.

"You're good," he said quietly, his voice carrying an edge of admiration that definitely shouldn't have made her stomach flip. "But everyone slips eventually. And when you do…" He let the threat hang in the air like mistletoe, except instead of promising kisses, it promised handcuffs. And not the fun kind. "It's just a matter of time," he added, his eyes never leaving hers. "And I've got nothing but time, Miss Martinez."

"That's sweet," Wren replied, tilting her head. "But maybe instead of playing hide and seek with murder weapons, you should focus on finding whoever's been stealing all the lawn decorations in the neighborhood. Mrs. Henderson's inflatable Santa went missing last week, and honestly? That seems more pressing." She gestured toward their window, where Mrs. Henderson's yard sat sadly Santa-less, looking like Christmas had forgotten to show up. "I mean, who steals Santa? That's the real crime here."

Warren's jaw tightened, but something flickered in his eyes—amusement? Interest? Whatever it was, it made Wren's pulse jump in a way that had nothing to do with fear and everything to do with really inappropriate timing.

The officers eventually filed out one by one, each giving the apartment one last sweeping look as if expecting an axe to suddenly materialize out of thin air. Wren wondered if they taught "suspicious glancing" at the police academy or if it was just something that came naturally with the badge.

After they left, Riley collapsed onto their couch, sending a shower of tinsel everywhere. "Well," she said brightly, "at least we didn't have to share our cookies. Though I guess offering snacks to the cops searching for evidence of our murders would've been pretty on brand for us." She picked up one of the cookies, examining it with newfound concern. "Maybe we should stick to regular shapes next time. These candy cane shanks might be a bit too on the nose."

Wren sank down next to her, adrenaline still coursing through her veins. "We need to leave," she said finally. "Like, pack-our-bags-and-become-professional-nomads kind of leave." She glanced around their apartment, at all the holiday decorations that suddenly seemed like evidence of a life they couldn't keep living. "I'm thinking Canada. They have good healthcare, legal weed, and at this point, I think we both need therapy."

"Can we at least finish decorating the tree first? It looks sad, and I feel like going on the run with unfinished Christmas decorations is bad luck." Riley reached for another ornament, this one mercifully just a regular bauble without any hidden weapons. "Plus, I refuse to let Detective McDreamy ruin our Christmas. Even if he does have unfairly good bone structure for someone trying to put us in prison."

Wren threw a piece of tinsel at her friend's head, but couldn't quite suppress her smile. Trust Riley to be thinking about their Christmas decorations in the middle of a crisis.

Though she had a point about Warren's bone structure.

It really was criminal.

20
WREN

HOW TO FLEE THE COUNTRY WITHOUT LOSING YOUR FRENCH PRESS

December 24, 2014
10:45 P.M.

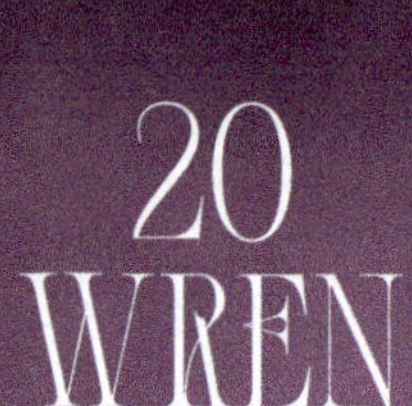

No one ever taught you what to bring when packing for life on the run. There wasn't exactly a "Fugitive Essentials for Dummies" book available, though Wren was starting to think maybe there should be. She stared at her open closet, trying to decide if someone actively fleeing from murder charges needed four different types of black hoodies.

"Do you think Canada has good coffee?" Riley asked from where she was sprawled on Wren's bed, surrounded by what looked like the aftermath of a department store explosion. "Because I refuse to become a fugitive somewhere with subpar caffeine. I have standards."

"Pretty sure when you're running from multiple murder charges, coffee quality becomes a secondary concern. But they have Tim Hortons, it's supposed to be good," Wren replied, though she made a mental note to pack their French press anyway. Even potential prison couldn't make her drink instant coffee.

The house felt different now like the police search had stripped away their illusion of safety. Every creak made them jump, every passing car headlight sent them diving for cover. Riley had already stress-cleaned the entire kitchen twice, though Wren suspected that had more to do with destroying evidence than actual hygiene.

"You know what's weird?" Riley said, stuffing shirts into her bag with the same careful abandon she'd used to hide murder evidence. Which was to say, about as carefully as a tornado organizing a closet. "I keep thinking about when we tried to start a vegetable garden and killed all the tomato plants. Like, how did we manage to become successful murderers when we couldn't even keep plants alive?"

"Pretty sure tomatoes are harder to kill than ex-boyfriends," Wren muttered, then paused. "Though that might be the darkest thing I've ever said, and considering our recent activities, that's saying something."

They worked methodically, gathering only what they absolutely needed. Burner phones went into one bag, along with what was left of their emergency cash stash

- which was suspiciously low after Riley's last snack run. Wren packed their fake IDs, carefully made by a guy who didn't ask questions as long as the money was good.

"Should we bring the TGPMC shirts?" Riley held up one of their murder club t-shirts. "I mean, they're evidence, but they're also really cute."

"We are not bringing merchandise from our murder club while actively fleeing from murder charges."

"But they're limited edition!"

"Because we're the only ones who have them!"

One last cleaning came next. They wiped down every surface that might hold fingerprints, though Riley got a bit carried away and started cleaning things that definitely couldn't be fingerprinted, like their houseplants.

"Can't be too careful," she insisted when Wren pointed this out. "What if they develop some kind of plant DNA testing?"

"I'm pretty sure Mr. Ficus here isn't going to testify against us in court."

Around midnight, Wren called Megan. The conversation was carefully coded - they'd learned that much at least. "Hey, remember that favor you owed us? For that… problem we helped you with? We need to cash it in."

Megan understood immediately. After all, nothing bonds people quite like helping dispose of an abusive ex. "Tell me what you need."

The plan was simple enough: Megan would come over at 2 AM with her car. Riley and Megan would take the Jeep and drive off, hopefully drawing any surveillance with her. Then Wren would slip out in Megan's car and pick up Riley at their designated meeting spot, where Megan would discreetly drop her. They'd be gone before anyone realized the switch.

"It's like a magic trick," Riley said as they waited. "Now you see us, now you don't. Though usually magic tricks involve fewer potential life sentences."

At 1:55 AM, they did one final sweep of the house. Wren paused in the living room, looking at their half-decorated Christmas tree. It looked sadder now, like it knew they were abandoning it. The murderous snowman ornament seemed to wave goodbye.

"We should take him," Riley said, following her gaze. "He's like our mascot now."

"We are not taking evidence-based Christmas decorations on the run."

Megan arrived right on schedule, her headlights off as she pulled into their driveway. She didn't ask questions when she saw their packed bags, just gave them both a tight hug. "Be careful," she whispered. "And delete my number when you're done."

Riley and Megan got into the Jeep and Riley took a deep breath before starting the engine. "See you on the other side," she said with a weak smile. "Try not to get arrested before I get back."

"Try not to hit anyone with the car this time," Wren shot back. "We really don't need to add to our body count right now."

She watched as Riley drove off, and sure enough, a dark sedan pulled out from down the street to follow her. Wren felt a mix of relief and worry - relief that their plan was working, worry about all the ways it could still go wrong.

Twenty minutes later, Wren slipped into Megan's car, a Subaru Outback that definitely hadn't been used in any crimes. Yet.

As she pulled out of the drive with the headlights off the house looked smaller in the rearview mirror, like it was already becoming a memory.

Wren drove in silence to the meeting spot, an abandoned gas station that had gone out of business years ago. Its faded signs advertised prices that hadn't been relevant since the 90s, and the only customer was a very determined opossum going through the ancient dumpster.

Riley showed up fifteen minutes later, practically falling into the backseat. "That," she announced, "was the most stressful drive of my life. And I once hit someone with my car on purpose."

"Please stop bringing that up when we have witnesses present," Wren sighed, but she couldn't hide her relief at seeing Riley safe.

They said goodbye to Megan with quick hugs and quicker instructions about retrieving her car later. "Remember," Wren told her, "if anyone asks—"

"I haven't seen you, don't know where you went, and definitely didn't help you flee from justice," Megan finished. "My mother will vouch for my whereabouts, no questions asked. I've watched enough crime shows to know the drill."

As they pulled onto the interstate, the reality of their situation finally hit. They were actually doing this - becoming fugitives, leaving everything behind. The highway stretched out before them like a promise or a threat, depending on how you looked at it.

"So," Riley said from the backseat, already rummaging through their snack bag, "Canada, eh?"

"Did you just make a Canadian joke while we're actively fleeing from murder charges?"

"I'm stress-joking! It's how I cope!" Riley pulled out a bag of gummy bears. "Besides, we should practice our Canadian accent. You know, for authenticity."

"Pretty sure that's not how immigration works."

They stopped at a 24-hour gas station just past the state line, paying cash for gas and coffee that tasted like it had been brewing since the Carter administration. The fluorescent lights made everything look slightly unreal, like they'd stepped into some parallel universe where college girls regularly went on the run from murder charges.

"Should we get more snacks?" Riley asked, eyeing the candy aisle. "I feel like being a fugitive probably burns a lot of calories."

"We literally just started driving."

"Yeah, but what if we get hungry in Canada? Do they

even have Red Bull there? These are important logistical concerns, Wren."

The radio crackled to life as they got back on the road, and Wren's heart nearly stopped when she heard their names: "Authorities are searching for Wren Martinez and Riley Thompson, wanted for questioning in connection with multiple murders in the Riverside area…"

Riley reached forward and snapped it off. "Well," she said after a moment of heavy silence, "That was quick. I guess we're officially famous now. Though I was kind of hoping it would be for something cooler, like inventing a new type of coffee or winning a reality show."

"Pretty sure 'suspected serial killers' isn't the kind of famous most people aim for."

"Hey, exposure is exposure. Though your mom's definitely going to be mad we missed Christmas dinner. Being serial killers is one thing, but breaking holiday plans? Unforgivable."

The sun was just starting to peek over the horizon as they crossed another state line. Wren glanced at Riley in the rearview mirror and found her friend had finally fallen asleep, clutching a bag of gummy bears like it was a teddy bear. The morning light made everything look softer, almost peaceful like they were just two friends on a road trip instead of fugitives running from multiple murder charges.

Wren adjusted her grip on the steering wheel, trying not to think about Detective Warren and the way he'd looked at her. Running from the law was complicated enough without adding inappropriate attraction to the mix. Though she had to admit, as far as people trying to arrest her went, he was definitely the most attractive.

"Stop thinking about the hot detective," Riley mumbled from the backseat, apparently not as asleep as she seemed. "That's, like, Stockholm Syndrome or something."

"I wasn't—"

"You had your 'thinking about the hot detective' face on. I can tell because you get this little crease between your eyebrows, like you're trying to decide if handcuffs count as flirting."

Wren focused on the road ahead, deliberately not thinking about handcuffs or detectives or anything except getting as far away as possible. The highway signs pointed toward Canada, each mile taking them further from their old lives and closer to… well, they weren't quite sure what yet.

But at least they had each other. And gummy bears. And their French press, because even fugitives deserved good coffee.

Though maybe they should have brought the murderous snowman ornament after all. It seemed wrong to leave their only Christmas decoration with good taste in weapons behind.

Evidence
January 13, 2015
Case Number 27b57
Detective: W.W.

CHASING THE CANADIAN DREAM (AND RUNNING FROM MULTIPLE

December 26, 2014
3:45 AM

Riley stared out the window at the endless stretch of highway, watching reflectors flash by like tiny stars. She'd already counted seventeen trucks, played "I Spy" with herself until she ran out of things to spy (turns out highways at night weren't exactly packed with visual variety), and gone through their snack supply twice. The thing about being a fugitive was that nobody ever mentioned how boring it could be.

"Did you know Canada has different flavors of chips?" she said, breaking the silence that had settled over them like a heavy blanket. "Like, ketchup-flavored chips. That's either brilliant or horrifying. I can't decide."

Wren's hands tightened slightly on the steering wheel. "Is now really the time to be critiquing Canadian snack options?"

"Well, if we're going to be fugitives there, we should at least know what we're getting into, snack-wise." Riley shifted in her seat, trying to find a comfortable position. "Plus, I heard they put gravy on french fries. With cheese curds. That's either genius or a cry for help."

"Pretty sure our current situation is more of a cry for help than their food choices."

They'd been driving for hours, taking back roads whenever possible and avoiding major highways. Riley had pulled up directions to various border crossings on her phone, looking for the smallest, most remote options. "What about this one?" she asked, pointing to a spot on the map. "It's basically in the middle of nowhere. Probably staffed by, like, one very bored person and maybe a moose."

"A moose would make a very effective border guard, now that you mention it," Wren mused. "Though I guess that would depend on its stance on international fugitives."

The conversation drifted to what they'd do once they made it across. Riley suggested opening a wellness center called "Murders & Meditation" before quickly adding "Kidding!" when Wren shot her a look that could have frozen hell.

"We could open a café," Wren said after a while.

"Something small, quiet. The kind of place where nobody asks questions about your past."

"Or a bookshop," Riley added. "But like, with weed…and cupcakes! And maybe some light crime on the side. Nothing major, just enough to keep our skills sharp."

"We are not starting a crime-based bookshop."

"Fine, but I'm still naming the cupcakes after murder weapons. 'Death by Chocolate' is getting a whole new meaning. And don't even get me started on our 'Killer Coffee' menu." Riley sat there looking like she'd just pitched the next Silicon Valley startup, rather than another half-baked[1] scheme to combine crime and capitalism.

Around 4 AM, exhaustion finally won out over paranoia, and they pulled into a motel that looked like it had last been updated when disco was still popular. The neon sign buzzed and flickered, missing enough letters to spell out "V CA CY" in a way that seemed ominously appropriate.

Riley handled check-in, channeling her best "definitely not running from murder charges" smile at the clerk, who looked about as interested in their presence as a cat at a dog show. They paid cash, used fake names (Riley had chosen "Rose Tyler" because "if we're going to use fake names, we might as well be obvious about it"), and made their way to a room that smelled like decades of

---

1   Riley would like to take a moment to appreciate the genius of "half-baked" appearing in a sentence about both baked goods and marijuana. She considers this peak literary achievement, even if the authors claim it wasn't intentional.

questionable life choices.

"Home sweet temporary hideout," Riley announced, dropping their bags on a bed that creaked ominously. She pulled out their emergency joint - because apparently, even their weed needed qualifying adjectives now - and lit up, watching the smoke curl toward the water-stained ceiling.

"Remember that road trip we took sophomore year?" she asked, passing the joint to Wren. "When we got lost and ended up at that weird museum of sock puppets?"

"You mean when you insisted you knew a shortcut and we ended up three states over?" Wren took a hit, her expression softening slightly. "That sock puppet of Abraham Lincoln still haunts my nightmares."

"Good times," Riley sighed. "Back when our biggest crime was trespassing in abandoned buildings for Instagram photos."

She watched as Wren got up to check the window again, probably for the hundredth time. There was something different about her friend lately - a distraction in her eyes, a tension in her shoulders that went beyond their current fugitive status.

"Okay, spill," Riley said, propping herself up on one elbow. "What's going on in that very illegal head of yours?"

"Nothing. Just… thinking about the border crossing." But Wren's eyes drifted toward the window again and Riley would bet her last bag of emergency gummy bears that she was thinking about a certain detective with annoyingly good bone structure.

"You're thinking about Warren," Riley accused. "You know, that crease is going to become a permanent fixture on your face if you don't cut that out."

"I am not—" Wren stopped, sighing. "It's complicated."

"Yeah, developing a crush on the guy trying to arrest us for multiple homicides definitely qualifies as complicated."

"It's not a crush," Wren protested, but her cheeks flushed slightly. "It's just… there was something about the way he looked at me. Like he could see right through all the lies, but maybe he didn't want to."

"Great, so not only is he trying to arrest us, he's also giving you meaningful looks. That's like, double illegal." Riley took another hit from the joint. "Though I guess it would make a great story for the grandkids. 'How did you meet? Oh, he was investigating us for multiple murders.'"

The weed was starting to kick in, making everything feel slightly surreal. The motel room's ugly wallpaper seemed to breathe ever so slightly, its faded floral pattern dancing in the dim light. Riley stared at it until the flowers started looking suspiciously like tiny crime scenes.

"This isn't what I thought being a fugitive would be like," Riley said suddenly, her voice cracking slightly. "I mean, not that I spent a lot of time thinking about it before, but still. We're literally running for our lives, living in sketchy motels, and I can't even tweet about it because social media is how they catch people now."

"Pretty sure our murder club activities voided our social media privileges."

"But I had so many good murder puns saved up!"

Wren moved to sit next to her on the bed, their shoulders touching. "We'll figure it out," she said softly, but there was a tremor in her voice that Riley had never heard before.

"You don't know that," Riley shot back, weeks of fear and anxiety suddenly bubbling to the surface. "We could get caught tomorrow, or next week, or in ten years when we've finally perfected our Canadian accents and opened that weed-and-cupcake bookshop/cafe combo."

"No, I don't know that," Wren admitted, and the honesty in her voice made Riley's chest tight. "But I know I wouldn't change a single thing we've done. Not one murder, not one midnight cleanup, not one terrible pun you made while hiding evidence. Whatever happens— prison, Canada, or that questionable bookshop idea you won't let go of—I'll be right beside you. That's what best friends are for. Helping you hide bodies and never leaving your side."

She squeezed Riley's hand, her voice softening. "It's you and me, babe. Till the very end, no matter what that end looks like."

Riley launched herself at Wren, wrapping her in a fierce hug that nearly knocked them both off the bed. They clung to each other, both pretending not to notice the way their eyes had gone glassy with tears. When they finally pulled apart, they were wearing matching watery smiles—the kind reserved for best friends who'd accidentally started a murder club and somehow ended up impossibly closer for it.

They sat in silence for a while, passing the joint back and forth until it was nothing but a tiny stub. The bathroom light cast weird shadows on the wall, making their silhouettes look like strangers.

"We should try to sleep," Wren said finally. "We've got a long drive tomorrow."

They pushed a chair against the door and laid extra pillows along the bottom, because apparently, paranoia made excellent interior decorators. Riley insisted on leaving the bathroom light on - "for ambiance," she claimed, though they both knew it was because complete darkness felt too vulnerable now.

Riley lay awake, listening to Wren's breathing in the other bed. Every car that passed made her tense up, expecting sirens or shouting or whatever happened when fugitives got caught. She'd seen enough crime shows to have a general idea, but TV never showed this part - the quiet moments of fear, the way your whole world could shrink down to a single motel room with questionable carpeting.

Around dawn, Wren started tossing in her sleep, muttering something that sounded suspiciously like "Warren" before jerking awake with a gasp.

"Bad dream?" Riley asked softly.

"Just the usual. Being chased, getting caught, realizing I showed up to class naked." Wren's attempt at humor fell flat. "Though the naked part might have been about Warren."

"Okay, we definitely need to work on your taste in men."

They packed up as the sun started to rise, erasing any trace of their presence from the room. Riley looked at their reflection in the bathroom mirror - two college girls with dark circles under their eyes and the weight of multiple homicides on their shoulders. Not exactly the graduation photos their parents had hoped for.

The map showed a small border crossing about six hours away, marked by nothing but a thin line and a lot of empty space around it. "If we're lucky," Riley said as they loaded the car, "they'll be too busy looking for us in all the wrong places."

Wren just nodded, gripping the steering wheel like it was the only thing keeping her grounded. Maybe it was.

A police siren wailed somewhere in the distance, making them both jump. Wren pressed down on the gas, and Riley watched their motel disappear in the rearview mirror, along with any chance of a normal life.

But at least they had each other. And weed. And the promise of ketchup-flavored chips in their future.

Though Riley still wasn't sure if that last part was a pro or a con.

22
RiLEY

ARMED, DANGEROUS, AND
IN DESPERATE NEED OF PANCAKES

December 27, 2014
8:15 A.M.

The worst way to start your morning, Riley decided, was to the sound of your own face being described on national television. She blinked awake to find Wren already up, staring at the motel room's ancient TV with an expression that suggested she'd just seen a ghost. Or, more accurately, seen their mugshots being broadcast across America.

"—authorities are searching for Wren Martinez and Riley Thompson, two college students wanted for questioning in connection with multiple murders," the newscaster announced with practiced gravity. "The women were last seen—"

Riley lunged for the remote, nearly falling off the bed in her haste to silence the TV. But the damage was done. Their grainy college photos stared back at them from the screen – Riley's from some party where she'd thought flower crowns were still cool, and Wren's from what appeared to be a particularly aggressive yearbook photoshoot.

"Well," Riley said, trying to inject some humor into the situation, "at least they used a photo where your bangs looked good."

"This isn't funny, Riley." Wren was already throwing their belongings into bags with the kind of efficiency that suggested she'd been mentally rehearsing this moment. "We need to go. Now."

They snuck out through the motel's back entrance, past a dumpster that had definitely seen better decades and a cat that gave them a look that said it had seen worse crimes than theirs. Riley couldn't help but wonder if cats could be called as witnesses in court. Though given this one's judgment, they'd probably be doomed.

The drive was tense, with both of them jumping at every passing car like they were starring in their own particularly anxious action movie. Riley kept checking her reflection in the side mirror, wondering if she looked like someone who had multiple murders on their conscience. She wasn't sure what that was supposed to look like, but she doubted it involved a shirt that said "Gangster

Napper" in faded letters.

"Do you think they'll make a true crime documentary about us?" she asked, mostly to break the suffocating silence. "Because if they do, I hope they use better photos. That flower crown was clearly a cry for help."

"As I've said before, our entire situation is a cry for help," Wren muttered, but Riley caught the ghost of a smile on her face.

Around mid-morning, their growling stomachs forced them to stop at a small diner that looked like it hadn't updated its menu since the Cold War. The sign outside advertised "Best Pie in Three Counties!" which Riley thought was oddly specific but also kind of charming.

The waitress who greeted them had the kind of smile that suggested she'd seen everything and judged most of it. Riley ordered pancakes because if she was going to potentially get arrested, she wanted her last meal to involve maple syrup.

That's when she noticed him – a man in a flannel shirt who kept glancing their way with increasing interest. At first, she tried to convince herself he was just being creepy in the normal way, not the "I recognize you from the news" way. But then she saw him reach for his phone.

"Wren," she whispered, trying to keep her voice steady. "Don't look now, but Flannel Man is either about to ask us out or call the cops, and I'm not sure which would be worse right now."

"We need to go," Wren said, already sliding out of the booth and tossing cash down on the table. "Now."

They bolted, leaving behind half-eaten pancakes and probably several concerned citizens who were definitely calling the police. Riley's heart was doing some sort of complicated gymnastics routine in her chest as they sprinted to the car.

"That," she gasped as they peeled out of the parking lot, "was not how I wanted to end my relationship with those pancakes. They deserved better. We deserved better."

After putting some distance between them and the diner, they stopped at a thrift store to change their appearance. Riley found herself trying on different personas along with the clothes – a baseball cap and oversized sweater that screamed "college student who definitely hasn't killed anyone," a pair of thick-rimmed glasses that made her look like someone who would lecture you about indie films.

"How about this?" she asked, modeling a look that could best be described as 'suburban mom who's very concerned about GMOs.' "Think it says 'definitely not a fugitive'?"

"I think it says 'we need to hurry up before someone recognizes us,'" Wren replied, but she was already paying for their selections – including a blonde wig for herself that Riley thought made her look like a very confused Taylor Swift impersonator.

Back on the road, every car that pulled up behind them felt like a potential threat. Riley kept track of them in a running commentary: "Blue sedan – probably just lost. Red pickup – definitely giving us the eye. Minivan

– unless it's full of SWAT team members in soccer mom disguise, we're probably okay."

The radio crackled with another news update about their case, and Wren quickly switched it off. But not before they heard "expanding the search" and "considered armed and dangerous."

"Armed and dangerous?" Riley scoffed. "The most dangerous thing about us right now is my caffeine withdrawal. Though I guess that's pretty lethal."

She was trying to keep things light, but the reality of their situation was starting to sink in. They weren't just running anymore – they were being hunted. Every person they passed could be the one to recognize them, every stop could be the one that leads to their capture.

The gas gauge needle was hovering dangerously close to empty, a silent but persistent reminder that they couldn't run forever. Or at least, not without regular fuel stops.

"We need gas," Wren said, voicing the thought neither of them wanted to acknowledge.

Riley nodded, adjusting her new baseball cap and checking her reflection one last time. "Well," she said with forced cheerfulness, "at least we look cute for our potential arrest."

The gas station loomed ahead, and Riley couldn't help but wonder if this would be where their luck finally ran out. Though really, she thought as they pulled up to the pump, their luck had probably run out somewhere around their first murder.

Everything after that was just borrowed time and very questionable life choices.

176

Josh
Nik
Greg
Dylan   Zach
Blythe   Nick
Tyler   Scott
Nathan
Michael
Peter
Jacob
RIP
Maurice

23

WARREN

9:30 AM

*T*he thing about hunting murderers was that it rarely involved the kind of dramatic car chases and shootouts you saw in movies. Usually, it was just Detective Bill Warren, sitting in his motel room at an ungodly hour, surrounded by enough paperwork to kill a small forest. The photos of Wren Martinez and Riley Thompson stared up at him from their case files – college yearbook pictures that looked more like sorority recruitment shots than mugshots of suspected serial killers.

He'd been over the evidence so many times he could recite it in his sleep. Josh Bennet, the first victim, disappeared on Halloween night. Then came Nik, Greg, Dylan, and more – each death more elaborate than the last, each victim sharing a common thread: they were all abusive men who had somehow slipped through the system's cracks.

Warren's coffee had gone cold hours ago, but he barely noticed as he took another sip. His eyes kept drifting back to Wren's photo. There was something in her expression, even in this staged college picture, that spoke of sharp intelligence and carefully contained defiance. He remembered the way she'd looked at him during the house search like she was daring him to figure her out.

His cell phone's sharp ring cut through his thoughts.

"Detective Warren? This is Officer Chen from the Highway Patrol. We've got a possible sighting of your suspects at Pete's Diner off Route 16. Customer recognized them from the news broadcast, said they took off in a hurry."

Warren was already grabbing his jacket. "How long ago?"

"Less than an hour. They headed north."

North. Toward the border. Of course.

He had been following their trail and wasn't far. But the drive to the diner gave him too much time to think. He found himself replaying every interaction with Wren, analyzing each word, each look. The way she'd stood her ground during questioning, her composure never cracking even as he'd pushed harder. Most people broke under that kind of pressure, but Wren? She'd pushed back.

"Focus," he muttered to himself, gripping the steering wheel tighter. She wasn't just some fascinating puzzle to solve – she was a suspect in multiple homicides. The fact that those homicides had arguably made the world a better place was irrelevant. Murder was murder.

Except… was it? Fifteen years of police work had taught him that justice and law weren't always the same thing. He thought of his sister, killed by an abusive boyfriend who walked free on a technicality. How different would things be if someone had stopped him first?

The diner looked exactly like he'd expected – all chrome and neon, trying desperately to cling to its 1950s glory days. The waitress who'd called it in, Sabrina according to her name tag, had the weary look of someone who'd seen too much drama over too many cups of coffee.

"They seemed nice enough at first," she told him, refilling his cup without asking. "Ordered pancakes, kept to themselves. But then Jimmy over there" – she nodded toward a man in flannel – "started looking at them funny, and next thing I know, they're bolting like they've seen a ghost."

Warren interviewed Jimmy next, who confirmed recognizing them from the morning news. "The blonde one, she kept watching everyone like she was counting exits. And the other one, with the purple hair? She had this look about her. Like she was ready for anything to happen and was just waiting for it."

Back in his car, Warren spread out his map, marking their likely route. If they were heading for the border, they'd want to avoid major crossings. His fingers traced the smaller checkpoints, trying to think like they would. Like she would.

He couldn't deny it anymore – his fascination with Wren had crossed a line. There was something about her that drew him in, made him want to understand her motivations, her mind. It was more than just solving a case; it was solving her.

"Damn it," he muttered, running a hand through his hair. He was too old, too experienced to be acting like some rookie caught up in the allure of a dangerous suspect. But every time he thought about her, he remembered that moment in her house – the way she'd met his eyes, the electricity that had passed between them. Like she knew he understood, even if he couldn't admit it.

The radio crackled with updates from other units. They were closing in, setting up checkpoints, watching the borders. It was only a matter of time before someone spotted them again. Warren should have felt satisfied, triumphant even. Instead, he felt... conflicted.

He pulled back onto the highway, heading north. The morning sun cast long shadows across the road, like nature's own arrows pointing him toward his targets. Toward her.

"This ends today," he told himself firmly. But even as he said it, he wondered what ending he was really hoping for.

The road stretched out before him, empty and full of possibilities. Somewhere ahead, Wren and Riley were running, probably planning their next move. He had to admire their resourcefulness, their determination. In another life, they might have made excellent detectives themselves.

Warren checked his rearview mirror, half-expecting to see Wren's knowing smirk reflected back at him. Instead, he saw only the road behind him, growing distant like all the certainties he used to have about right and wrong.

He pressed down on the gas, choosing to focus on the chase rather than the complications waiting at its end. After all, that's what good detectives did – followed the evidence, caught the bad guys, and kept things simple.

Too bad nothing about Wren Martinez was simple.

The radio crackled again: another possible sighting, this time at a gas station near the state line. Warren changed direction, trying to ignore the way his pulse quickened at the thought of seeing her again.

Some hunts were about justice. Others were about something else entirely.

He was starting to wonder which one this was.

24
WREN

WARREN'S HOT, BUT NOT HOT ENOUGH FOR PRISON TIME

2:45 PM

Running from the law really messed with basic survival needs. Like getting gas. Or using the bathroom. Or trying not to have an inappropriate attraction to the detective hunting you down. Wren was currently failing at all three as she pulled into a small gas station off the highway, the needle hovering dangerously close to empty.

"I'll grab snacks," Riley announced, already heading toward the convenience store. "Try not to look suspicious."

"Try not to buy the entire candy aisle," Wren called after her, but Riley was already through the door, probably making a beeline for the gummy bears she claimed were "essential fugitive fuel."

The afternoon sun cast long shadows across the parking lot as Wren started pumping gas. She was calculating how far they could get on a full tank when movement caught her eye – a black sedan pulling into the lot. Her heart stopped as she recognized the driver.

Warren.

Their eyes met across the parking lot, and time seemed to freeze. She could see the exact moment recognition hit him, watched his expression shift from tired detective to focused predator. It was unfairly attractive, which was absolutely not what she should be thinking about right now.

Wren yanked the gas nozzle out of the tank, probably breaking several safety regulations but figuring that was the least of her crimes at this point. She sprinted toward the store, her boots slapping against the pavement in rhythm with her racing heart.

"He's here," she gasped as she burst through the door, finding Riley contemplating different flavors of beef jerky like they had all the time in the world. "We need to go. Now."

"Original or teriyaki?" Riley asked, then registered Wren's expression. "Oh shit. Him him?"

"No, the other detective chasing us across state lines," Wren grabbed Riley's arm. "Yes, him!"

They rushed back outside, but Warren was already out of his car, moving toward them with the kind of determined stride that probably got him a lot of dates when he wasn't pursuing murder suspects. Not that Wren was noticing things like that. Definitely not.

Her hands shook as she fumbled with the keys, adrenaline making her usually steady fingers clumsy. Warren's voice rang out across the parking lot: "Stop right there!"

"Yeah, because that always works," Riley muttered as they scrambled into the car. "Has anyone in the history of being told to stop actually stopped?"

Wren had just gotten the key in the ignition when her door suddenly yanked open. Warren stood there, his hand on the frame, looking down at her with an expression that made her stomach do complicated things. Up close, she could see the stubble on his jaw, the intensity in his eyes, the way his breath came slightly faster from the chase.

"Miss Martinez," he said, his voice low and far too appealing for someone about to arrest her. "Going somewhere?"

Time seemed to slow down. Wren knew she should be terrified – she was literally face to face with the man trying to put her in prison – but instead, she felt that same electric current she'd sensed during the house search. From Warren's slightly widened eyes, she could tell he felt it too.

"You don't really want to catch me, do you?" she said softly, leaning closer. His grip on the door loosened slightly, surprise flickering across his face. She took advantage of his momentary distraction to slam the door shut and hit the gas.

They peeled out of the parking lot in a way that would have made Fast & Furious proud, leaving Warren sprinting back to his car. Riley turned around in her seat to watch him through the back window.

"Okay, but like… he's kind of hot when he's all determined and chase-y," she commented. "In that 'could definitely arrest us but might buy us dinner first' kind of way."

"Can you maybe not try to sell me on the man trying to put us in prison?" Though she had just been practically drooling over him herself.

Wren took a sharp turn onto a narrow road, hoping to lose Warren in the maze of back streets. His headlights appeared in their rearview mirror, persistent as her inappropriate attraction to him.

"I'm just saying, if we're going to get caught, at least it's by someone with good bone structure." Riley couldn't help adding.

They wove through increasingly remote roads, the chase becoming a dangerous dance of sharp turns and near misses. Warren stayed right behind them, his car a constant presence in their mirrors. Wren had to admire his determination, even as she tried to shake him.

"He's not giving up," Riley said, her earlier humor replaced by genuine fear. "What do we do?"

Wren spotted a dirt road leading into dense woods and made a split-second decision. The car bounced violently as they hit the uneven ground, branches scraping against the windows like nature's own warning system. Behind them, Warren's sedan struggled with the terrain, slowly falling behind.

When his headlights finally disappeared, Wren drove a bit further before pulling into a secluded clearing. The silence that fell was deafening after the chaos of the chase. She could hear both their ragged breathing, the tick of the cooling engine, and the pounding of her own heart.

"Well," Riley said finally, "I guess this means I don't get any jerky."

Wren let out a slightly hysterical laugh. "We nearly got caught, and you're worried about snacks? What am I saying, of course you are."

"Hey, proper nutrition is important when you're on the run! Though I guess prison probably has a meal plan." Riley's attempt at humor fell flat as her voice cracked. "We can't keep doing this, Wren. He's going to catch us eventually."

"No, he won't." But even as she said it, Wren couldn't stop thinking about Warren's face when he'd caught up to them at the gas station. There had been something there, beyond just the determination of a detective doing his job. A recognition, maybe. An understanding.

They drove through the night, sticking to back roads and avoiding any signs of civilization. Riley eventually fell asleep, but Wren stayed alert, her mind replaying that moment with Warren over and over. The way he'd looked at her, the electricity between them, the slight hesitation in his grip on the door.

It was ridiculous to be attracted to someone who was actively trying to arrest her. Completely insane. Definitely a sign that she needed therapy.

"You're thinking about him again," Riley mumbled, apparently not as asleep as she seemed. "It's the crease again."

"I do not have a crease," Wren protested, but she caught herself smoothing her forehead anyway. "And I'm not thinking about him. I'm thinking about… border crossing strategies."

"Sure, and I bet those strategies have nothing to do with tall, dark, and legally obligated to arrest us?"

Wren focused on the road ahead, deliberately not thinking about Warren's stubble or his voice or the way his presence seemed to fill any space he occupied. They needed to find somewhere to lay low, somewhere to regroup and plan their next move.

"We'll head north," she decided. "Find a small town where no one watches the news and—"

A police siren wailed in the distance, making them both jump. Wren pressed down on the gas, heart racing again. Whether she was running from Warren or her feelings about him was becoming increasingly unclear.

Though really, both options probably ended in handcuffs.

"I heard that thought," Riley said, and Wren realized she'd said that last part out loud. "And I'm judging you so hard right now."

Sometimes Wren wondered if being caught would be less stressful than dealing with her best friend's commentary on her questionable taste in authority figures.

Probably not.

25
RiLEY

THE CHAPTER WHERE WE DO SOMETHING REALLY STUPID (AGAIN)

11:45 P.M.

You know what sucks? High-speed chases are a lot less glamorous than movies made them look. Riley cursed as she yanked the steering wheel to avoid yet another police car. They were taking turns during their high-speed chase, you know, because nobody ever mentioned how much your arms hurt from all the desperate maneuvering. Or how the sirens started to sound less like "wee-woo" and more like a really aggressive EDM remix of your impending arrest.

"You know," she said, taking another turn so sharp it probably violated several laws of physics, "when I imagined going out in a blaze of glory, I was thinking more 'epic musical number' and less 'getting chased by the entire police force.'"

Wren's knuckles were white where she gripped the dashboard. "Pretty sure our musical number days ended when we started our murder spree."

Red and blue lights painted their faces in alternating flashes of panic as more police cars joined the pursuit. Riley had lost count somewhere after five, though really, anything more than zero was probably too many when you were trying to avoid prison.

"On your left!" Wren shouted, and Riley swerved to avoid a police cruiser that had tried to cut them off. The move sent them fishtailing dangerously close to the guardrail.

"Thanks," Riley gasped, steadying the wheel. "Though maybe next time lead with 'cop car' instead of sounding like we're in a Marvel movie."

"Pretty sure superhero movies have fewer murders."

"Depends on the movie. Isn't that right, Deadpool fans?" Riley said in a weird voice as she stared off into the distance, making a face.

"What are you doing?"

"Breaking the fourth wall, isn't it obvious? I was giving my best Jim Halpert face."

They could see a bridge ahead, a familiar silhouette dark against the night sky. Below, the lake stretched out like spilled ink, the same kind of waters that had kept their secrets all these months. The same kind of waters that might now keep them.

Riley felt a strange calm settle over her as they approached the bridge. It was like everything had been leading to this moment – every murder, every close call, every late-night planning session fueled by Red Bull and questionable life choices.

"You thinking what I'm thinking?" she asked, glancing at Wren.

"That we should've joined the swim team instead of starting a murder club?" Wren replied drily.

"Besides that." Riley's lips twitched. Even now, facing what might be their last moments, they couldn't help but fall into their familiar pattern of banter.

The Jeep screeched to a halt at the bridge's center, the move so sudden it sent them both lurching forward. Through the rearview mirror, they could see the police cars forming a blockade, their sirens wailing like banshees. Spotlights swept across the bridge, turning night into harsh, artificial day.

"You know," Riley said as they scrambled out of the car, the cold night air hitting them like a slap, "I always thought if I died young, it would be from something cool. Like fighting a shark, or choking on a hot dog at a competitive eating contest."

"Your priorities remain concerning until the very end," Wren replied, but she was smiling as they climbed onto the bridge's railing, the metal cold beneath their hands.

The police were shouting commands now, their

voices carried away by the wind. Riley thought she could see Warren among them, his figure distinct even at this distance. She wondered if he was looking at Wren, if there would always be that unfinished story between them — the detective and the murderer who might have been something else in another life.

"Guess this is what they mean by 'ride or die,'" Riley said, her voice steadier than it had any right to be as she gripped the railing.

Wren let out a sound that was half-laugh, half-sob. "Pretty sure this qualifies as both."

The spotlights were getting closer, the shouting more urgent. Below, the water looked impossibly dark and deep, promising either escape or ending — maybe both. The wind whipped around them, carrying the echo of every choice that had led them here.

"Ready?" Riley asked, reaching for Wren's hand.

"No," Wren answered honestly, taking it anyway. "But when has that ever stopped us?"

They shared one last look — best friends, partners in crime, literal ride-or-dies. In Wren's eyes, Riley saw everything they'd been through: that first Halloween night with Josh, all the murders that followed, the late nights planning, and the early mornings running. She saw the friendship that had turned them from college students to vigilantes, from normal girls to something else entirely.

"Hey, Wren?"

"Yeah?"

"If this is it… if this is our last adventure…" Riley's

voice cracked. "I wouldn't want to jump off a bridge with anyone else."

Wren squeezed her hand, tears mixing with her smile. "We had a good run, didn't we?"

"The best. Worth every murder." The tears sliding down Riley's cheeks were blown away in a gust of wind.

"Together?" Wren's voice was sure and steady.

"Always."

And then they jumped.

The fall seemed to last forever and no time at all, the wind whipping their hair, their joined hands tight enough to bruise. Riley's last thought before hitting the water was that she really should've waterproofed her vape.

The impact knocked the breath from their lungs, the cold shocking their systems like a thousand tiny knives. The dark water swallowed them whole, wrapping around them like a final embrace. Their hands were torn apart by the force, and for a moment, Riley felt completely alone in the darkness.

Above, the bridge's lights grew dimmer as they sank deeper, becoming nothing more than distant stars in an endless night. The cold numbed everything – their bodies, their thoughts, their fears. It was almost peaceful, in a terrifying sort of way.

Riley's last conscious thought was that at least they'd gone out on their own terms. No handcuffs, no prison cells, no separating them. Just the two of them and the dark water, keeping their final secret.

The surface of the lake settled, ripples smoothing

out until it was as still as glass. On the bridge, the sirens continued their wail, the lights still flashed, but below, there was only silence.

And somewhere in the depths, two best friends either found their ending or their escape.

Though really, maybe those were the same thing all along.

EPILOGUE

OUR REDEMPTION ARC
(SPONSORED BY NETFLIX)

["Bad Guy" by Billie Eilish begins playing]

But they didn't die.
Turns out crime doesn't pay...
but TikTok does.

...Two hospital beds, side by side. Riley and Wren handcuffed to their rails, both giving weak thumbs up to the camera. Riley's heart monitor spelling out "YOLO" in its peaks. A newspaper headline visible: "Murder Besties Survive Leap, Detective Warren First on Scene for 'Rescue'"...

...Matching orange jumpsuits and carefully staged

mugshots. Riley somehow managing to make prison lighting look good. Wren rolling her eyes but secretly nailing her angle...

...Fanmail flooding the prison. Letters from women across the country. #FreetheMurderBesties trending on Twitter.

...Gloria Allred stepping out of a sleek car, designer briefcase in hand. The media circus begins...

...Courtroom sketches going viral. Riley and Wren in matching pantsuits, their "innocent" faces practiced to perfection. Detective Warren testifying, unable to keep his eyes off Wren. Twitter explodes with "enemies to lovers" fan edits...

...Magazine covers: "The Killing Cuties: Justified or Psychopaths?" "Murder Besties Tell All!" "From True Crime Fans to True Crime Stars" "Detective and Former Fugitive: A Modern Love Story?"...

...Five years later: Riley and Wren leaving prison, squinting in the sunlight, wearing designer jumpsuits because fashion houses literally fought to dress them. Warren waiting by his car, no longer a detective but somehow looking even better in civilian clothes...

...First date: Warren and Wren at a coffee shop, both trying not to mention that the last time they saw each other, he was testifying at her trial. Riley watching through the window with binoculars, "for safety"...

...Warren proposing at the bridge where they jumped, because he's dramatic like that. Riley filming it for their YouTube channel, "The Girlie Pop Chronicles"...

...The wedding: Wren in white, Warren in a tux, Riley as maid of honor wearing a shirt to the reception that says "My Best Friend's a Killer"...

...Book deals. Movie rights. A Netflix documentary series titled "Killer Friendship Goals"...

...Final shot: The girls on their new podcast set, "Murder Was the Case (That They Gave Me)," wearing matching "Sorry About the Murder Thing" t-shirts from their merchandising line. Riley taking a hit from a gold-plated vape while Wren adjusts her microphone. Warren in the background wearing an "I Married the Suspect" shirt, looking both proud and slightly concerned...

Some people say crime doesn't pay. But those people probably didn't have a good social media strategy.

[Roll credits]

BONUS CHAPTER
RILEY

THE UNEXPECTED SIDE EFFECTS OF
STARTING A MURDER CLUB

March 24, 2015
9:40 AM

Prison had a way of making fame feel surprisingly inconvenient. Like right now, as Riley stared at the mountain of letters their guard had just dumped on her bunk with all the enthusiasm of someone delivering potentially radioactive waste. Which, given their fanbase, wasn't entirely out of the question.

"I think our fan club is multiplying," Riley announced, holding up a pink envelope that seemed to be shedding glitter like a disco ball in distress. "Either that or we've been nominated for Murderer of the Year. Do they have awards for that? They should."

Wren looked up from her own stack of letters, her expression suggesting she was reconsidering every life choice that had led to this moment. "Please tell me you're not actually considering a career in professional murder."

"Of course not," Riley replied, already reaching for another envelope. "I'm considering a career in murder-adjacent consulting. You know, for tax purposes."

The guard had delivered their latest batch of fan mail with the kind of resigned expression that suggested he'd read a few letters himself. Their cell was starting to look like a particularly concerning post office, with piles of letters sorted into what Riley called their "murder mail management system."

"Love letters go in the pink pile," she explained, tossing another envelope onto a growing stack. "Hate mail goes in the trash, unless it's really creative – then it goes in our 'Greatest Hits' collection. And anything asking for autographs gets its own special pile because apparently being convicted murderers makes us celebrities now."

"Your organizational skills are as concerning as your priorities," Wren muttered, but she was fighting a smile as she opened another letter. "Oh look, someone sent us prison survival tips. Number one: assert dominance by winning a fight on your first day."

"Been there, done that," Riley waved dismissively. "Though I maintain that tripping and accidentally headbutting someone totally counts as winning a fight."

They worked through the pile methodically, with

Riley providing dramatic readings of the more entertaining letters. There were marriage proposals (worrisome), requests for their "club's" services (more worrisome), and one very detailed letter about someone's cat that seemed to have been sent to the wrong address entirely.

"Hey, this one's actually kind of sweet," Riley said, holding up a carefully handwritten note. "This woman left her abusive boyfriend after reading about us. Says we gave her the courage to stand up for herself." She paused, something softening in her expression. "Though hopefully, she means metaphorically and not in the 'hit him with a car' way."

"We're terrible role models," Wren sighed, but she took the letter to read herself.

"Speak for yourself," Riley replied, already opening another envelope. "I think we're great role models. We taught valuable life lessons like 'actions have consequences' and 'don't be an abusive asshole or you might end up in a woodchipper.'"

The next letter contained a series of poorly drawn hearts and what appeared to be song lyrics about vigilante justice. Riley immediately started humming them to the tune of "Die Young," while Wren muttered something about their legal team definitely not approving of their "Greatest Hits" becoming actual hits.

"We should start a band," Riley suggested, arranging the letters into a makeshift music stand. "The Jailhouse Rockers. Or maybe Murder She Wrote, except we actually did the murders."

"Pretty sure that would violate several terms of our eventual parole."

Their sorting was interrupted by a guard bringing in a small package, which immediately set off all of Wren's survival instincts. Riley, however, dove for it like a kid on Christmas morning – if Christmas involved potentially dangerous packages from unstable fans.

"Please be careful," Wren warned as Riley tore into the wrapping. "Remember what happened with the glitter bomb last month?"

"Hey, that was festive! Besides, the guard's eyebrows grew back eventually."

The package contained what appeared to be someone's ex-boyfriend's class ring, along with a note explaining how the sender had "taken inspiration" from their club and wanted to offer "support from the outside." There was also a lock of hair that they both agreed to pretend they hadn't seen.

"Okay," Riley said slowly, carefully setting the package aside. "Maybe we should be more specific about not actually wanting people to follow in our footsteps. You know, add a 'don't try this at home' disclaimer or something."

"Because that always works so well on YouTube videos?"

They spent the day going through their favorites, compiling what Riley called their "Greatest Hits of Murder Mail." There was the letter written entirely in emojis, the elaborate prison break plan that seemed to be based entirely on watching Orange is the New Black, and the oddly specific request for their measurements "for historical accuracy."

"You know what's weird?" Riley said, lying back on her bunk and holding a letter above her head like she was studying ancient texts. "We probably did more for women's rights by being terrible examples than we ever would have by following the law."

"I wouldn't be surprised, it's been done by women all throughout history."

"Yeah, sometimes the patriarchy needs a little push. Or a shove. Or possibly a gentle nudge off a roof."

As they reached the bottom of the pile, Riley found one last letter – simple white envelope, neat handwriting, no hearts or glitter or suspicious substances. She opened it carefully, her usual dramatic flair falling away as she read.

"This one's different," she said quietly, and something in her tone made Wren look up. "It's from a girl who says we helped her realize she deserved better. Not by killing anyone, but by showing her that sometimes you have to be your own hero, even if that means breaking some rules."

"Or several laws," Wren added, but she was smiling.

"Details," Riley waved dismissively, but she folded the letter carefully and tucked it away. "Though maybe we should start replying with less murder-adjacent advice. You know, suggest therapy instead of homicide, that kind of thing."

"How responsible of you."

"I know, right? Prison's really helping with my

personal growth. Though that might just be the cafeteria food."

"You know what this means, don't you?" Riley said as they finished organizing. "We're basically folk heroes now. Like Robin Hood, but with better hair and more creative disposal methods."

"Pretty sure Robin Hood didn't have a fan club asking for murder advice."

"His loss, really. Though I guess 'steal from the rich' is easier to explain than 'maybe don't hit people with cars unless absolutely necessary.'"

As lights out approached, Riley tucked their favorite letters into their designated hiding spot — a loose brick in the wall that had probably seen its fair share of contraband over the years. The last one she put away was the simple white envelope, the one about being your own hero.

"Hey, Wren?"

"Yeah?"

"Think we'll get this much fan mail in Canada?"

"We are not starting an international branch of the murder club."

"Fine," Riley sighed dramatically, flopping onto her bunk. "But can we at least get matching maple leaf tattoos? You know, to commemorate our eventual escape and definitely successful border crossing?"

Wren threw a pillow at her head, but she was

laughing. Because really, what else could you do when your murder club had accidentally started a movement and your fan mail needed its own filing system?

At least prison gave them plenty of time to work on their reply letters. Though maybe they should avoid using red ink — some things were a little too on the nose, even for them.

BONUS CHAPTER
WREN

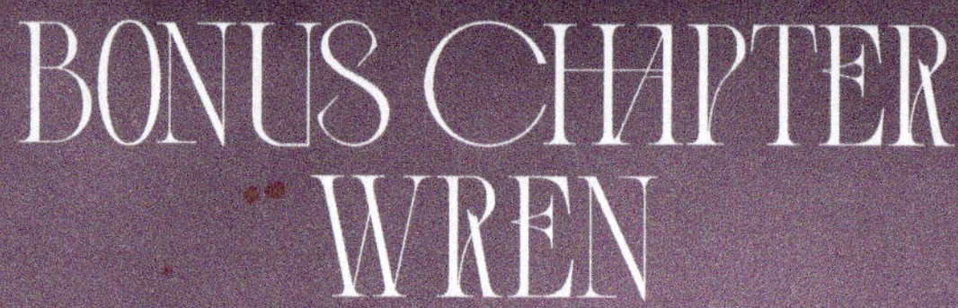

THE BRIDGE CHAPTER 2:
ELECTRIC WEDDING BOOGALOO

May 7, 2021
7:30 PM

Sunlight glinted off the bridge's metal railings, catching Wren's eye as she approached. Warren stood at the center, looking suspiciously well-dressed for what he'd claimed was "just a regular date." His hands were stuffed in his pockets, and he had that particular expression she'd learned to recognize from their days of cat-and-mouse - the one that meant he was planning something.

What she didn't know was that approximately fifty feet away, Riley was crouched in the bushes with a professional camera setup that definitely hadn't come from their YouTube revenue. "Operation Proposal Capture is a go," she whispered to her audience, adjusting what appeared to be Warren's old surveillance equipment. "Our subject is displaying classic pre-proposal behavior - sweaty palms, nervous fidgeting, and what appears to be at least three pocket checks for the ring."

"You're being weird," Wren announced as she reached Warren, eyeing him suspiciously. "And not your normal weird. Like, special occasion weird."

Warren's laugh came out slightly strained. "Can't a guy just want to take his girlfriend to a meaningful location?"

"The meaningful location where I once jumped off a bridge to escape arrest? By you?" Wren raised an eyebrow. "Should I be concerned about history repeating itself?"

"Actually," Warren started, then seemed to lose his nerve. He shifted his weight, hand moving to his pocket again. "I wanted to talk about us."

Something in his tone made Wren's stomach drop. "Oh god, is this where you finally admit that dating a former murderer is too complicated? Because I've seen the way people look at us in restaurants, and—"

"What? No!" Warren looked genuinely confused. "Why would you think—"

"Because you've been acting strange for weeks!" Wren threw up her hands. "And every time someone recognizes me in public, you get this look—"

"That's because I've been trying to figure out how to propose without someone live-tweeting it!"

The words hung in the air between them. From the bushes, Riley whispered "Plot twist!" to her camera.

"You..." Wren blinked. "What?"

Warren ran a hand through his hair, looking equal parts frustrated and fond. "This isn't how I planned this. I had a whole speech prepared about how this bridge represents our story - how watching you jump made me realize I couldn't imagine a world without you in it, even if that meant giving up everything I thought I knew about right and wrong."

"Are you..." Wren's voice caught as Warren pulled out a small box. "Is this actually happening?"

"Well, I'm already halfway through ruining the surprise, so..." He opened the box, revealing a ring that caught the sunlight like a promise. "I had this whole romantic moment planned, but since we've never done anything the normal way—"

He didn't get to finish because Wren had thrown herself at him, kissing him with enough force to make him stumble back. His arms wrapped around her waist automatically, the ring box pressed between them.

When they finally broke apart, Warren was grinning. "So... is that a yes?"

"No, I just felt like making out on a bridge for fun," Wren replied, rolling her eyes even as she smiled. "Of course it's a yes, you dramatic—"

Confetti exploded around them, making them both jump. Eco-friendly, biodegradable confetti with wildflower seeds rained down, promising future blooms where they stood. Warren nearly dropped the ring in surprise.

"YES!" Riley burst from the bushes, camera held high. "Finally! Do you know how long I've been planning this? The confetti cannons alone took weeks to coordinate!"

"Riley," Wren said slowly, "did you hijack our proposal?"

"Excuse me, I enhanced your proposal," Riley corrected, still filming. "And may I say, the dramatic argument into surprise proposal was chef's kiss - totally unexpected, great content for the channel."

"You're supposed to be in Canada," Warren pointed out, though he was fighting a smile.

"Please, like I'd miss this." Riley adjusted her camera. "Besides, someone had to document it properly. Your surveillance skills are good, babe, but my cinematography is better."

Wren looked between her best friend and her now-fiancé, shaking her head. "You know most people don't have their former murder accomplice film their proposal."

"Most people are boring," Riley declared, then spun the camera around to face herself. "Hey Girlie Pop Chronicles fam! Your girl just captured the proposal of the century - former detective marries former murder suspect, proving that love really can conquer all. Even multiple homicide charges."

In the background, Warren slipped the ring onto Wren's finger, pulling her close for another kiss. The confetti settled around them like snow, each piece carrying the promise of future flowers - beauty growing from the place where their story had once seemed to end.

"And that's a wrap on today's video!" Riley announced to her camera, positioning herself to get Warren and Wren kissing in the background. "Don't forget to like and subscribe for more updates on your favorite reformed murderers! Next week: wedding planning with a criminal record - do we go with prison orange or traditional white?"

Wren broke away from Warren just long enough to call out, "We are not involving our YouTube channel in wedding planning!"

"That's what you think!" Riley sang back, still recording. "But seriously, folks, isn't love beautiful? Even when it starts with a high-speed chase and ends with eco-friendly confetti cannons. Actually, especially then."

The sun was setting now, casting long shadows across the bridge where two stories - one of escape, one of romance - had now merged into something new. Warren held Wren close, both of them laughing as Riley continued her commentary about "star-crossed lovers who crossed all the right lines."

After all, some love stories needed a little murder, a little justice, and a best friend with surprisingly good aim with confetti cannons.

EMBER'S ACKNOWLEDGGEMENTS

To my best friend - who not only helped write this book but inspired it. Don't worry, officer, that's not a confession. She's never actually murdered anyone for me. That I know of. That I can legally confirm. That would hold up in court. But she did help me hide a body... of work. (See what I did there? Literary humor. Totally innocent.)

To Shazara, Dread, Knight Owl, and Lavender - my personal cheer squad who listened to me ramble about this book with the patience of saints and the enthusiasm of accomplices. Thanks for pretending my constant book talk wasn't more annoying than an ex-boyfriend with boundary issues. Your support is everything, and your alibis are solid.

To my husband - who has mastered the art of plausible deniability and never asks why I'm googling "fastest decomposition rates" at 3 AM. Your unwavering support and strategic lack of curiosity make you the perfect partner in crime writing. Thanks for always being my alibi (I mean, loving spouse).

To my dad - who helped brainstorm the perfect murder plans with a concerning level of expertise. I promise to only use this knowledge for literary purposes. Mostly. (Note to FBI agents reading this: He's just really good at true crime shows. Nothing to see here.)

To my hometown - thanks for being just creepy enough to inspire a murder story, but not creepy enough to inspire actual murder. Your ratio of abandoned buildings to working streetlights is truly inspiring.

To me - because if you can't appreciate yourself, who will? Besides, someone had to write this book, and all the other authors I asked were suspiciously busy. Or disappeared mysteriously. (Just kidding! Legal team, please don't quit.)

Special thanks to:

- The Walgreens night shift workers who never ask questions
- That one suspicious raccoon who minded its business
- Various true crime podcasts that definitely didn't teach me anything useful
- The makers of face masks, because self-care is important even during felonies
- My lawyer, who advised me not to write these acknowledgments
- Coffee, vapes, and the persistent fear of failure that fuels all writers

No thanks to:

- Josh (you know what you did)

- Whoever designed those cheap plastic devil horns
- The person who decided shovels shouldn't be more ergonomic
- That one cop who definitely thinks this book is suspiciously well-researched

Remember: Any similarity to actual murders is purely coincidental. Probably. Maybe. No comment.

(P.S. - If anyone asks, we were all at the library that night. Every night. Forever.)

CALLIE'S ACKNOWLEDGEGEMENTS

I only have one other person to give thanks to.
My beloved partner,
the one man who didn't make it on the list.

ABOUT THE AUTHOR
EMBER EAST

When she's not locked away in her writing cave, cackling maniacally at her own jokes, Ember can be found wrangling her three feral children, who may or may not be the result of a genetic experiment gone wrong. Her husband, bless his heart, has learned to nod and smile politely when Ember starts rambling about her latest literary masterpiece, all while secretly wondering if he married a mad genius or just a plain ol' madwoman.

Ember's writing journey began when she realized that the voices in her head weren't just a sign of impending insanity but rather a goldmine of comedic material. She firmly believes that laughter is the best medicine, unless you're suffering from a broken bone or a severe case of the runs. In those cases, please seek professional medical help.

ABOUT THE AUTHOR
CALLIOPE ZETSUBŌ

Calliope spends her days surviving being a mother, watching the minutes crawl by. When the spawn sleeps, she writes or plays video games. She's constantly on a call with her long distance partner, so good luck getting her on the phone.

Her writing journey started as a young child trying to escape trauma. As an adult living with an alphabet soup of mental disorders and chronic illnesses, she's still just trying to escape into her dark fantasy worlds.

Her friends and partner will tell you she brings light to every room she walks in, and her laughter is infectious. Yet she'll still look you straight in the eye, and pull out an uno reverse.

ALSO BY

EMBER EAST

The First Witch Series
Daughter of Realms
Princess of Realms
Queen of Realms

The Haphazard Hocus Pocus Collection
A Magic of Magic and Magic
A Reckoning of Rogues and Rescues

As Ember Everstar

The Shadows of Nemorsa Series
Whisper of Shadows

www.ingramcontent.com/pod-product-compliance
Lightning Source LLC
Chambersburg PA
CBHW070418310726
48977CB00003B/739